Dalton went rigid at Evangeline's words. What he wanted from her would shock her. What he wanted from her shocked *him*.

"Angie, I knew what I wanted from you the first time I saw you."

Her brows furrowed. "What?"

"You heard me."

"Yes, I did. I meant, what do you want?"

She couldn't be that naive. Not with those eyes. "What any man wants from a woman who looks like you do."

She just waited. "Well?" she said at last. "Are you going to tell me what you want or not?"

"No... I'm going to show you."

Dear Reader:

Welcome to Silhouette Desire - provocative, compelling, contemporary love stories written by and for today's woman. These are stories to treasure.

Each and every Silhouette Desire is a wonderful romance in which the emotional and the sensual go hand in hand. When you open a Desire, you enter a whole new world - a world that has, naturally, a perfect hero just waiting to whisk you away! A Silhouette Desire can be light-hearted or serious, but it will always be satisfying.

We hope you enjoy this Desire today - and will go on to enjoy many more.

Please write to us:

Jane Nicholls
Silhouette Books
PO Box 236
Thornton Road
Croydon
Surrey
CR9 3RU

Errant Angel
JUSTINE DAVIS

SILHOUETTE Desire

*First published in Great Britain in 1995
by Silhouette Books, Eton House, 18-24 Paradise Road,
Richmond, Surrey TW9 1SR*

© Janice Davis Smith 1995

*Silhouette, Silhouette Desire and Colophon are
Trade Marks of Harlequin Enterprises II B.V.*

ISBN 0 373 05924 8

22-9509

Made and printed in Great Britain

JUSTINE DAVIS

lives in San Clemente, California. Her interests outside of writing are sailing, doing needlework, horseback riding and driving her restored 1967 Corvette roadster —top down, of course.

A policewoman, Justine says that years ago, a young man she worked with encouraged her to try for a promotion to a position that was, at that time, occupied only by men. "I succeeded, became wrapped up in my new job, and that man moved away, never, I thought, to be heard from again. Ten years later he appeared out of the woods of Washington state, saying he'd never forgotten me and would I please marry him? With that history, how could I write anything but romance?"

Other Silhouette Books by Justine Davis

For the proprietor of
Tom's Garage…

The real angel in my life

Prologue

"We have no choice."

"We're shorthanded."

"She's the only one available."

The words were as gloomy as the clouds that swirled around them while the group sadly agreed. They turned as one to look at the boss, who let out a sigh. That alone told them he'd about reached the end of his rope, a rope pulled tight for too long and far too often by their errant problem child.

"Very well," he answered at last. "We will try once more."

"Maybe it will be all right," someone else put in hopefully. "Somehow, even when she does things…differently, they seem to come out right in the end."

There was a grumble of voices as they argued over that optimistic interpretation.

"She's not that bad," the hopeful one insisted. "You know her heart is true, she just gets...impulsive sometimes. And she was rather young when we recruited her. It's not her fault that she didn't have as much life experience as some of the others."

The rest of the group snorted—as much as they were capable of—in disdain.

"Enough."

They stopped, and turned their attention once more to the boss.

"Perhaps we've been going about this the wrong way," he went on. "Perhaps in trying to control her, we've made a mistake. Humans are unpredictable."

"Now *that's* an understatement," somebody muttered, earning an uncomfortable moment of the boss's attention.

"I think," he continued, "that this time we shall—how do they say it?—let her run."

"I think they say," somebody else muttered, "give her enough rope to hang herself."

"Perhaps," the boss agreed. "Or perhaps she will prove herself instead."

"You mean you're really going to turn her loose? No safeguards, no limitations?"

There was a pause before the answer came. "None except those necessary to protect her."

A low, collective whistle rose from the group. Only once before had the limitations been suspended, and the result had been...well, unexpected, to say the least. It was the reason they were shorthanded now; they'd lost their very best, but they found it hard to mourn the loss when it had taught them much about human love and joy.

"If we're going to do it," the hopeful one said, "we'd better do it now. That child is headed for big trouble."

"Yes," the boss said, focusing on the hopeful one. "You'll be her contact for this mission."

"Me?"

"Yes. Everyone else seems to expect her to fail. That's not what we're about."

A rustling rose from the group as the rest of them shifted uncomfortably; there was too much truth in the boss's words.

"All right," the hopeful one agreed, although they all knew she had little choice in the matter. And it was an honor, of sorts, to be put in charge.

Even if past history showed it might be somewhat like being in charge of an out-of-control circus.

One

What on earth?

Evangeline lifted her head, pressing one hand against her chest. What on earth, she repeated silently, was this odd feeling? This pressure, this constriction, this awful tightness?

In the depths of her mind, a memory stirred, but it was gone before she could put a name to it. The squeezing sensation increased, until she felt as if something vital would burst under the strain. She looked around her, but nothing had changed. She was still alone in the quiet, wet darkness of the little California town a few lonely miles over the hills behind Santa Barbara, on a midnight-deserted street where even the dogs had taken refuge from the rain.

Her fingers curled as she reached toward the golden chain around her neck. But before she could touch the oddly shaped pendant that hung from the chain, the distant mist in her mind parted, and she knew what the feeling was.

Pain. She was feeling pain.

She was so startled that she nearly slipped on a patch of rain-slick pavement. Pain?

"Impossible," she murmured. She never felt pain. They'd made sure of that. Especially not this kind, the heart-wrenching, gut-level agony of emotions ripped to shreds.

She looked around again, but saw nothing unusual, no explanation for this unexpected sensation. The drugstore she stood in front of was dark. So was the café at the end of the block. The only sign of life at all was a light on upstairs over the auto repair shop across the street.

She tried to focus on the pain, tried to sense the source, but the feeling itself was so fierce, so strong, that it overwhelmed all else.

She reached again for the pendant that hung from the gold chain around her neck. It warmed in her hand, gave off an eerie golden glow, but nothing else happened.

"Great," she muttered. "The line's busy."

She waited, not very patiently; it was hard, in the face of this unrelenting ache, to be stoical. At last the pendant thrummed gently. She nearly snapped the inquiry out.

What took you so long?

The answer formed chidingly in her mind. *Tut, tut, my dear, it wasn't that long.*

Easy for you to say. I've got a problem here.

So we sensed. Whatever is that odd sensation?

It's pain, oh mighty one.

Sarcasm does not become you, Evangeline. Besides, that's impossible. You know you can't be injured.

Not physical pain. This is different. Emotional.

Oh?

Interest filtered through. The concept of emotional pain, of pure, human heartache, had always fascinated her bosses, since they never experienced it themselves. It had been a very long time since she'd felt that kind of pain, but she remembered, and the memories were more vivid than any recollection of mere physical discomfort.

She tightened her fingers around the pendant as she went on.

I can't find the source. It's so overpowering, I can't even determine a direction.

You've always been very sensitive in that area.

Her brow was furrowed now.

I still can't pin it down. How can I accomplish my mission if I can't even *find* my mission?

She could have sworn she heard a sigh. *Hopefully not the same way you usually do.*

She would have blushed if they hadn't removed that capability, as well. She knew they were referring to her sometimes reckless approach, and tactics that had caused them much stress on more than one occasion. Then, before she could come up with a suitable—or even unsuitable—comeback, they gave her an answer that puzzled her.

Actually, you shouldn't be sensing pain from your target. He's not feeling pain right now, emotional or otherwise. The boy is much too angry.

Then what am I getting? It's awful. Like someone whose soul is caving in on him.

Him?

She hesitated before going on.

Yes, it is a man. I can tell that much. He *must* be my mission. He's in agony.

No. It's the boy. You know that, we sent you all the information.

I know, it's just that—

No, Evangeline. Please, for once, tend to business.

But—

No.

It was flat, it was determined, it was an order, and if she hadn't known it was impossible for them, she would have said they were tired. She gave up for now.

I understand, she sent.

The connection faded. Quickly. Maybe they *were* tired, she thought. Of her, she added glumly. As if it was her fault people sometimes didn't react the way she thought they would. Well, if they didn't like the way she did her job, then they could fire her. After all, she hadn't asked for this, they'd come to her. Of course, she hadn't had many options at the time....

Now that the communications link was gone, the pain came rushing back. It seemed to roll over her from her left, and instinctively she looked in that direction. And saw again the single light glowing in the window over the repair garage.

She had taken several steps before the stern order she'd been given brought her up short. She stood there in the dampness, not really feeling the chill. It didn't take her long—it never did—to rationalize it out. She obviously couldn't function through this haze of pain, so she had to find the source, didn't she? Maybe it was something she could fix quickly, and then get on with her work, as ordered.

She started off again, then hesitated again. They *had* been angry with her, the last time. She'd half expected them to pull her after that one. Not that it had been her fault that dying little girl's brother had been so awful. And she'd thought the punishment she'd doled out to him moderate enough—why shouldn't he spend a week hearing in his head what everyone was thinking about him? Besides, it had all come out right in the end.

And she couldn't bear this. She truly couldn't. Besides, she hadn't really said she'd give it up. She'd said only that she understood they wanted her to. She started toward the light.

Three Oaks Garage.

She stood looking up at the faded lettering over the high, roll-up door. The place looked old, as did most of the buildings of this small business district that was centered around the plaza where the three spreading old trees the town had been named for stood. She had no doubts now that she was in the right place; whoever was sending off those waves of anguish was here, close by. No doubt in the room with the light; no one who was feeling like this would be sleeping much.

She tilted her head back, staring up at the rectangle of light. She spared a second to hope that the bosses weren't monitoring her power usage, then closed her eyes and concentrated.

The darkness behind her eyelids seemed to swirl, then lessen, fading to gray. Slowly the image formed, wavered, then settled.

It was a small room, teetering on the edge of shabby. There were few furnishings; a narrow, neatly made bed against a far wall, a single armchair in front of a small television, on top of which was the only new touch in the room, an inexpensive VCR. Across a side wall was a sink, a small two-burner stove, and a waist-high refrigerator. Next to that was a door that led to a tiny, pocket bathroom.

The carpeting was worn to the threads in spots, and the curtains that hung at the single bank of windows were old and faded by the sun. Yet the room was painfully clean and tidy, with none of the clutter of day-to-day living. No dishes, no glasses, no newspaper casually tossed after reading. The atmosphere of the room was beyond austere, it was almost Spartan.

This visualizing was the hardest of her powers to maintain, and she knew she would be drained if she kept it up much longer. Still she concentrated, raising her fingers to her temples and pressing in a way she'd found helped her sharpen the images.

She sensed him then, sitting at a plain wooden table against the wall beneath the windowsill, and she shifted her concentration. She saw his hands first, strong, work-roughened hands with long, supple-looking fingers curled around the pen he held, an end gripped in each clenched fist. Gripped so tightly, as he stared at the sheet of paper in front of him, that his knuckles were white with tension.

Even as she watched, the plastic of the pen gave under his fierce grasp, snapping in two with a sharp, cracking sound. His head came up then, and he stared at the ruined pen in his hands with eyes that were full of rage, pain and, oddly, resignation. It was a combination so powerful she had to suspend the vision for a moment, for fear the pain would swamp her.

Resignation. The thought came to her suddenly: as if he'd expected nothing less from his own hands than destruction. And for the first time in longer than she could remember, she couldn't tell if the flash of intuition had come from the outside, as usual, or from within her. It had seemed different, but she hadn't had to rely on her own instincts for so long, she wasn't certain she would recognize them anymore.

Just as she wasn't certain about the odd feeling that flooded her as she looked at the man whose suffering had drawn her here. His hair was dark, long enough to brush over his shoulders, and somewhat shaggy. It gleamed in the light of the single lamp, as meticulously clean as the room he sat in. His shoulders were broad, his waist narrow, and he looked a bit too thin for his size, although there was no lack of muscle in the arms bared below the rolled-up sleeves of a faded chambray work shirt.

She looked again at his face, at the lean, strong jaw, the high, almost aristocratic cheekbones, the straight line of his nose. And she saw the scar, although it was nearly concealed by the thick fall of his hair over his forehead. It was a jagged, wicked mark, running from his right temple up into the hairline above his right eye.

Those eyes. She made herself look at them again, bracing herself for a flood of that incapacitating pain. There was so much darkness around this man that it almost startled her to realize his thickly lashed eyes were green, shadowed now, but a vivid green nevertheless.

The image shifted, wavered, and she knew she was going to lose it. She saw him throw down the broken pieces of the pen, saw them roll across the paper on the desk, coming to a stop below the scrawled salutation that was the only thing written on the page. He reached out and crumpled the paper into a shroud for the destroyed pen, and tossed them both into a metal can on the floor.

And the pain faded away. As if he'd tossed it into the can, as well.

With the loss of the pain, her focus shattered and she was once more out on the rainy street, staring up at the rectangle of light.

And she was exhausted. She always was, when she tried to use that particular talent for too long. She'd heard that some of the others found it easy, and she envied them. Nothing seemed to come easily for her.

But at least she could think now, of something other than that awful pain. She could go on and, as the bosses had said, "tend to business." Yet she stood still, heedless of the rain that was becoming heavy again.

Who was Linda? That had been the name he'd written at the top of the page. "Dear Linda." Then he'd stopped. Because the pain had started? Was she a lover, lost to him, this Linda who caused him such agony?

She felt an odd pang at the thought, a faint echo of the ache she'd sensed before. But again, she couldn't be sure of its origin, if it had indeed been his pain, or her own.

She nearly laughed at herself. Of course it wasn't her own pain; she never felt pain. But she did get tired, and she was tired now. That had to explain why she was suffering from this odd confusion. A little rest and she'd be fine. She'd better be, she had a lot to do tomorrow. In fact, she had more to do tonight, if the people whose lives she was about to drop into were going to accept the persona she was to present to them. It was time to get started.

But as she turned away, she couldn't help but look back at the window above her.

It was dark now.

"I don't know about you guys, but I think this text-book is as dull as dishwater."

Twenty fifteen-year-olds gaped at their new teacher, then turned heads to stare at each other in astonishment.

"So," Evangeline went on, "we're going to do this a little differently. History from a book is fine, but it's dead. History was made by living, breathing people, like you, and that's how it should be taught. So this—" she held up the heavy, ponderous text and grinned "—is history."

She dropped the book into the cavernous bottom drawer
of the desk at the front of the room and slammed the
drawer shut. A cheer went up from the room.

"Ms. Law?"

Evangeline nodded at the wide-eyed, concerned-looking
girl who sat in the front row. "Yes, Karen?"

"What will we study, then?"

"Who cares?" came a voice from the back of the room.

Jimmy, she thought. Jimmy Sawyer. Her mission.

His slouched, careless posture trumpeted his disinter-
est, not only in school but in life in general. Thin and gan-
gly, he wore ragged, baggy jeans rolled up above heavy,
black combat boots, a T-shirt with the logo of one of the
more rancorous rock bands, and a denim jacket with the
sleeves cut out. His sandy brown hair hung long over his
right ear, but was cut short on the left side, no doubt purposely, to draw attention to the dangling silver skull ear-
ring that pierced his left ear.

And anger radiated from him, until Evangeline was
amazed that one so young could contain it all. His foster
parents must be at their wit's end with him. But he had
every right to be angry at life, she thought. His entire
family—parents and a brother and sister—had been wiped
out six years before, in the crash of a plane en route to the
funeral of his grandfather, a plane he hadn't been on because he'd been sick and had to stay at home with a neigh-
bor. The report from the bosses had been strictly factual,
but the starkness of it only added to the poignancy; because he'd missed one funeral, he'd been the only one left
to go to all the others.

Knowing the battle for the boy's future had begun, she
echoed his question. "Who cares?"

"Yeah," chimed in another student. "At least we don't
have to read that boring stuff anymore."

The cheering erupted again, this time threatening to get out of hand. Evangeline lifted her eyes and scanned the room, giving each of the rowdy students a full second's look. They settled down, even as they looked around suspiciously, as if not sure themselves why they were being so cooperative. Even Jimmy straightened a little, although he didn't look happy about it.

"True, you won't have to read 'that boring stuff,'" she explained. "But you *will* learn. You'll learn not only what people did, but why. You'll learn what they felt, what drove them to do what they did."

Their cheer started to fade a little. She paused, looking out over the class again, stretching her senses, processing the information they brought her.

"How would you feel," she said casually, "if I told you the government has decided to put a tax on, say, music, but only for kids? Adults won't have to pay it when they buy a CD or a tape. Just kids. And not because they want the money—but just to show you who's in charge, who has the authority, just to remind you that you're only children, and they're the boss."

There was an instant of silence, then an outburst of outraged discussion.

"That wouldn't be fair," Karen protested from the front row.

"What would you do about it?"

"Fight it!" the girl exclaimed.

"Quit buying tapes," a boy beside her put in.

"Jimmy?" Evangeline lifted a brow at the boy. "What would you do?"

He seemed surprised to be called on. The bosses had told her that the previous teacher had been glad the boy was usually content to be sullenly silent. The older man had been intimidated by Jimmy's appearance and his attitude.

But surprised or not, the boy had a seditious answer ready on the tip of his tongue.

"Screw 'em," he said. "I'd smash their stuff and send it back to them in pieces."

Cheers and shock seemed to be about evenly spread throughout the room.

"Well, Jimmy," she said, grinning, "*that* is exactly what the men of Boston thought the night they dumped the East India Company's tea into Boston Harbor."

The boy looked startled, then embarrassedly pleased as cheers rose from his classmates. Evangeline felt a spurt of relief; if the boy could still be pleased at the approval of his peers, then he wasn't beyond redemption. Maybe, just maybe, this job would go right.

"She's kinda cool, really. Nobody's cut class for a week now."

Dalton MacKay glanced at the boy, hiding his surprise. Cool was not a word Jimmy often used in reference to school. He straightened up from under the hood of the old truck and looked at the boy, who was fiddling with the chain on his rather distinctive bicycle, a conglomeration of brightly colored parts that Dalton wasn't sure he wanted to know the origin of.

"Hand me that spark plug socket, will you?" he said. Jimmy hesitated, then reached into the open drawer of the big toolbox. When he handed him the right socket, Dalton gave the boy a smile as he fastened it on the ratchet. "Good. You remembered. So, why is this new teacher cool?"

Jimmy smiled almost shyly at the acknowledgment that he had remembered what Dalton had taught him last weekend. Then he shrugged. "She just is. I mean, instead of makin' us read that junk, and then just memorize a bunch of dates and stuff that don't mean anything, she...she makes it seem real. Like it was real people, who were pissed off and did something about it.''

Dalton reached down to yank the next spark plug. ''It was real people.''

''I know, but it never seemed like that before. She makes you think about how they felt, you know? Like we talk about something that's a big deal today, and she gets us all going, and then shows us how what we feel is exactly what they felt, back then.'' The boy grimaced. ''It's hard to explain.''

''I'd say you explained it just fine,'' Dalton said. ''Hand me that box of new plugs, will you?''

Jimmy scooped up the small carton from the neatly organized workbench and handed it to him.

''You'd like her, too,'' Jimmy said.

Not likely, Dalton thought. It had been a long time since he'd liked anybody. He only tolerated Jimmy hanging around all the time because he reminded him so much of himself at that age, full of anger and putting up a tough front to hide hurt feelings he wouldn't ever admit to having. He knew the boy had been orphaned young, had lived in foster home after foster home since, and he couldn't help the stirring of empathy he felt, despite his vow never to feel anything resembling closeness to anyone again.

Jimmy was looking at him expectantly and, trying to hide the weariness of another near-sleepless night, Dalton asked the question Jimmy was expecting.

''What makes you say that?''

''Well,'' Jimmy drawled, not disguising the bantering note in his voice very successfully, ''it could be because she's really awesome-looking. And she's not married.''

Dalton winced inwardly at the unsubtle words. But he didn't react outwardly; he remembered enough about being fifteen to know that any reaction would just egg the boy on.

Then, as if puzzled at himself, Jimmy added, "It's weird, though. I always thought blondes were the best looking, but she's got this hair that's like...like those trees up in the mountains, that change color this time of year, you know? Kind of red, brown and gold all mixed up together. And big brown eyes, all soft and gentle, like that fawn that came out of the hills last year."

Dalton blinked; for Jimmy, the description was tantamount to poetry. As if he realized that, the boy instantly lapsed back into insouciance. "She's kind of little, but she's built, too—long legs, nice little butt, great ti—"

"I get the idea," Dalton interrupted.

"Well, she's no older'n you are, and there aren't any single women as old as you around here—"

"Thanks," Dalton said dryly. "That's what I get for turning thirty."

"I just meant—"

"I know what you meant," Dalton said, more kindly this time.

After all, he thought as he bent over the fender of the old truck to begin installing the new spark plugs, how was the kid supposed to know that the absence of available women—or anyone else his age—was one of the attractions this little, out-of-the-way town held for him? People were abandoning small towns like this in droves, but he had searched this one out, looking for peace, not to forget, but to remember.

"I like things just the way they are, okay? The last thing I need is some woman cluttering things up."

Especially some long-legged woman with a nice little butt and brown eyes like Bambi.

"Yeah," Jimmy said, grinning widely now, "but this one drives an absolutely cherry '57 Chevy."

Dalton straightened up, curious now. "A what?"

"You heard me. It's red and white, in primo shape, and is it hot!"

"Two-door?"

"You got it. Bel Air hardtop."

One corner of Dalton's mouth quirked upward. "Two eighty-three, V-8?"

Jimmy's smile faded. "I... don't know. I mean, it sounds hot, but I..."

His voice trailed off in uncertainty, and Dalton remembered how hard it was at that age, when you'd worked so hard at that "cool, don't care" attitude, to admit there was something you didn't know.

Dalton shrugged easily. "That's why you're here, right? To learn?"

The boy's expression brightened. "I told her I liked cars, that you were teaching me about them, so she let me look at it this afternoon."

The boy seemed suddenly embarrassed, and Dalton felt a flash of trepidation.

"And?" he prompted.

"I..."

"Jimmy," he said warningly.

"I sort of...invited her over here today. I thought you'd like to see the car."

Dalton smothered a groan. He'd had a feeling he'd regret the day he let Jimmy start hanging around. He'd come here to be alone, not have everybody in town casually dropping by.

"Damn it, Jimmy," he began, but when he saw the boy's face change, when he saw the flash of fear in his eyes before that uncaring facade snapped back into place, he bit back the rest of his exclamation; it was like looking at an image of himself at fifteen, all the walls already in place, hiding the fear that had filled him. By twenty, those walls had been nearly impenetrable. If Mick hadn't come along—

He cut the thought off swiftly, with the ease of long practice. He heard the sound of a car approaching—one that obviously, from the healthy sound of the motor, didn't need his attention—but ignored it for the moment. Jimmy, he thought. Concentrate on Jimmy. He hadn't meant to scare the kid.

"Never mind," he said. "It's okay. I just had a lot of work to do today." He shrugged. "But it'll be here tomorrow. And how often does a guy get a chance to look at an 'absolutely cherry '57 Chevy'?"

Jimmy brightened up, and the practiced facade of indifference fell away. For a moment he looked like an average, excited fifteen-year-old boy. The boy Dalton had seen glimpses of, the boy the rest of Three Oaks would swear didn't exist. They saw only the troublemaker, the tough-talking, rough-dressing kid, and they shook their heads and muttered about what was wrong with kids these days. Just as, in another town much like this one, adults had once shaken their heads and spoken as if the words Dalton MacKay and delinquent were inseparable.

"You're not really mad, then?" Jimmy asked.

"No. Not really."

"Good," the boy said with relief. "Because here she is."

He turned, realizing he should have guessed what the source of that healthy thrum was. He couldn't help smiling when he saw what looked indeed like an "absolutely cherry" '57 Chevy, with the distinctive tail fins and the inimitable styling. The red-and-white car came to a halt, and the rumble of the powerful motor stopped. Dalton felt his smile widen; he'd always had a weakness for beautiful machinery, and this classic was all of that—perfectly straight, sleek and utterly spotless.

Then the driver's door opened, and a pair of legs that seemed to go on forever swung out. A woman stood up, a sweep of burnished auburn hair with golden highlights that danced in the sun falling forward as she tugged down a skirt that wasn't that short to begin with, but seemed that way because of the length of the shapely legs beneath. A gold shape he couldn't discern from here glinted against the skin below her throat.

Besides the legs and that incredible hair, the rest of her seemed to live up to Jimmy's advance billing, as well; she was petite, barely five-three, he guessed, but the womanly curve of hip combined with an eminently cuppable derriere was a potent combination. And speaking of cuppable, Dalton thought a little numbly, aware he was staring but somehow unable to stop, her breasts were more than nice, they were—

They were none of his business, he snapped at himself, straightening the fingers that had involuntarily started to curl at his thoughts, angry at his unexpected reaction. But she was, as Jimmy had said, awesome-looking.

Then she raised her head, looked straight at Dalton, and his heart slammed to a stop as his gut contracted fiercely. This was no fawn-innocent woman, despite the huge brown eyes. Those eyes had seen much, and held a bone-deep wisdom and gentleness he'd seen only once before in his life, in the eyes of the man who was the closest thing he'd ever had to a father. The man he'd killed as surely as if he'd taken a gun and blown his brains out.

Two

It *was* him, Evangeline thought, her breath stalling oddly in her throat. He seemed to be as stunned as she was. The moment their eyes had met she'd felt a rush of reaction from him, so confused and powerful she hadn't been able to sort out the emotions. Then he'd shut himself off, and she hadn't been able to read anything. Or perhaps it had been because she'd been dealing with an unexpected response of her own.

She didn't understand it. She shouldn't be reacting this way. Her vision that rainy night had been quite clear, so why was he so much more ... more everything, in person? And why did she feel this strange sensation in her chest, as if her heart had suddenly lost its rhythm and was trying madly to find it again?

He was taller than she would have guessed from what she'd seen that night, his dark hair not as shaggy-looking now that it was neatly combed, and he didn't seem quite so thin now that she was standing face-to-face with his leanly muscled body. But those incredible green eyes were unmistakable, although they were shuttered now, unreadable, even to her. This man had had a lot more practice than Jimmy at putting up walls.

When the boy had first mentioned Dalton MacKay, she'd thought it must be the man she'd seen; he did live over the garage, after all. And when Jimmy had told her more about him, she'd been nearly certain.

"About the only guy between eighteen and fifty in the whole damn town," the boy had said. "It's weird that he wanted to come here. Everybody else bails out of this pit stop as soon as they can."

Just like I'm going to.

The boy hadn't said the words, but he hadn't needed to; the words, the need, were clear in his eyes. As, she realized, was the hero-worship. She'd noticed it the first time the boy had begun to talk about Dalton MacKay.

It was the boy's talk about cars, and about the man whose name had once been known by thousands, that had prompted her to decide on the classic car. The quickest way to the boy's heart, she'd told the bosses. They had, somewhat to her surprise, agreed rather easily and produced the replication.

She'd known it was the right move the moment Jimmy had seen the Chevy; he'd lit up at the sight of it. His uncaring facade had fallen away, and he'd become uncharacteristically voluble in his enthusiasm. Then he had launched into extolling the virtues of the local mechanic—who was, it appeared, much more than he seemed.

"He drove at Indy, in the 500, can you believe it? Nearly won it as a rookie four years ago, and held first place up until his engine blew ten laps from the finish the next year. If it hadn't been for that crash . . .''

"Crash?" she'd asked, remembering the scar she had seen on the forehead of the man whose pain had overwhelmed her on that rainy night.

"Yeah. In the 500, two years ago. Dalton was hurt, and couldn't race anymore. It really stinks, because he would have won, I know he would."

And if he had, she thought as she looked at Dalton now, what were the chances that he'd be here, in this quiet little town, to become the idol that kept one angry teenage boy from blowing up entirely?

She knew the answer to that: zero.

She glanced at Jimmy; the boy's gaze was flicking from her to Dalton, somewhat uneasily.

"Er . . . Dalton, this is Ms. Law," he said finally, awkwardly. "The teacher I was telling you about."

Evangeline felt a tiny spurt of triumph. If the boy had been talking about her to his idol, then she was getting through. She hadn't expected results so quickly.

"I gathered," Dalton said.

Her breath caught again at the sound of his voice. And she didn't understand that any more than she did her other reactions to this man. In all her years in this work, nothing like this had ever happened to her.

"Isn't the car great?"

Jimmy's enthusiasm bubbled over, and satisfaction rippled through Evangeline at his innocent delight. This had been the right approach. The car had gotten her close to the troubled boy faster than anything else could have. Maybe at last she was getting the hang of this work. Maybe she could avoid a stern lecture on her sometimes chaotic methods this time.

"Yeah," Dalton agreed, turning his attention to the car. As she watched him, Evangeline was sure she had only imagined that sensation of relief as he had turned away from her. She had to have imagined it, because if she hadn't, then she was stuck with the problem of determining which of them it had come from, and she was having a little problem with that at the moment.

She heard Jimmy's excited chatter about the car, but her attention was fastened on the man beside him. She stared at him, reaching out with her senses; she had to know if he meant well by Jimmy, or had some ulterior motive for letting the boy hang around all the time. It was something she'd sadly learned over the years, that ulterior motives were often the norm rather than the exception, and she didn't like the idea of anyone using an already troubled boy—barely more than a child, really—for some reason of their own.

It wasn't working. She was blocked. She couldn't get through his formidable defenses, not from this distance. Those walls of his were too high, too thick; it was going to take more to read him. She was, she thought, sucking in a quick breath as the realization came to her, going to have to touch him. Only then could she find out what she needed to know. The idea disturbed her, and she wasn't sure why. But she knew it was the only way.

She moved toward them.

". . . love the red-and-white tuck-and-roll. And wait until you see the motor," Jimmy was saying, running around to the front of the car and moving as if to reach for the latch.

"Jimmy," Dalton said warningly, glancing at her.

The boy looked blank for a moment, then color tinged his cheeks. "Oh. Sorry." He looked at Evangeline, his eyes pleading. "Can I show him?"

"Of course you can." Good Lord, she thought. The town mechanic teaching the wild boy manners. Much of her wariness about the man's motives faded, but she still needed to be sure. She came up beside him as Jimmy fumbled with the hood latch.

Concentrating on thinking only of Jimmy, to screen the information she would get, she casually, as if accidentally, brushed against Dalton's arm. Her breath caught as skin touched skin; something seemed to leap between them, something hot, vivid and alive. For an instant she felt him stiffen, then, as casually as she had, he moved away. But it had been long enough.

For a moment the flood of images confused her; she thought by some glitch she was getting Jimmy directly instead. It seemed altogether too possible that she'd messed it up, as much trouble as she was having getting Dalton MacKay out of her thoughts. Then she realized it was only that the situations had been so alike—a temporary home with frustrated foster parents who were spread too thin and an abandoned boy who hid his fear behind a front of anger and sullen indifference.

She knew in that instant that Dalton MacKay had opened a tiny gap in his solid protective walls for no other reason than to try to help a boy whose feelings he understood all too well. And she knew, as well, how very hard it had been for him, to open up even that little bit.

But underlying everything she'd picked up from him was a vicious, draining sense of guilt, so powerful she could feel it tugging at her even now, after the contact had been broken. It almost overwhelmed the memory of that odd, electric little jolt that had raced through her at the touch of his skin against hers. Shaken, she had to turn away for a moment. Then Jimmy managed to release the latch, and she automatically looked up, following the movement as he lifted the hood.

She saw Dalton's eyes widen, and a low whistle escaped him. "Factory fuel injection!" he exclaimed. "These are really rare."

"I told you it was hot." Jimmy was grinning again.

Dalton glanced at Evangeline, hesitated, then asked, "The tranny's a four-speed close ratio, then?"

She saw the flicker of doubt and guessed he wasn't sure she could answer the question. She gave him a wry look.

"Yes. And it's all mine," she said. "Not borrowed from some husband or boyfriend back home."

He blinked, startled, then had the grace to look chagrined. "Sorry. I didn't think I was being that obvious. And I didn't mean to assume."

"That where there's a hot car, there's got to be a man involved?" Dalton shifted uncomfortably, and she relented. "It's okay. I'm used to...being different." If you only knew, she added silently.

"She likes baseball and football, too," Jimmy proclaimed, watching Dalton. "I told you she was cool."

Something she didn't recognize came into Dalton's gaze then, and incredibly, she felt heat rise in her cheeks. She was so startled she almost reached for the pendant, to ask what on earth was going on. She never blushed. It took emotions she wasn't supposed to have to blush.

"Yes," Dalton said slowly, answering Jimmy but looking at her. "Yes, you did."

A feeling she had never known filled her as she met his eyes—a sudden urge to run, to flee, to escape whatever was happening here. And she couldn't explain the impression she got that he was feeling the same way. Like two people who had opened doors on opposite sides of a room, to find the room in flames, she thought, wondering where the image had come from. But all that really mattered was this need to back away. Quickly.

"I—I have to go," she said. She sounded peremptory, she realized, and she hadn't meant to. Another oddity, she thought; she usually had complete control over her presentation; it was a necessity for her work. "I'm glad you like the car," she added lamely.

He looked as if he were about to say something, then stopped and merely nodded. He turned away, his expression showing her that her words had been a dismissal much sharper than she'd meant them to be. An awkward silence reigned as Dalton walked back to the truck he'd been working on without another word. He picked up a socket wrench and went back to work under the hood of the old truck.

"Uh," Jimmy began, obviously aware of the tension but uncertain—as she was, Evangeline thought—of the exact cause, "maybe you could bring it by again sometime. Dalton'd probably like to look closer at the motor, wouldn't you?"

He ended on a rising note, looking over at Dalton. The man merely shrugged, not looking up. Evangeline winced inwardly at the crestfallen expression that slipped over Jimmy's face.

"Maybe I will," she reassured the boy.

As she drove away she looked in the rearview mirror, seeing the two of them, together, yet as alone as any two people she'd ever seen.

And she wondered what on earth Dalton could possibly have done that could make him feel so much guilt it was nearly smothering him.

Are you guys doing something weird up there?
Whatever do you mean?

I mean, I know you aren't real happy with me, but if you're going to change the rules on me, I wish you'd at least let me know.

There was a moment of silence from them. She always thought of it as talking to "them," even though there was only one doing the actual communicating; it must be that ridiculous royal "we" they insisted on using. But she knew they were all listening. Especially when it came to her.

Evangeline tightened her grip on the pendant as she sat curled up in the big, overstuffed chair that took up one corner of the bedroom she'd rented from Mrs. Webster, mainly because it was across the street from the house where Jimmy lived. She waited, imagining them discussing what to tell her.

The answer came at last.

We told you that you had full freedom on this case.

That's not what I meant—not that it's not great, by the way, zipping that car up was the perfect way to get Jimmy's attention. But I meant the other stuff.

What . . . stuff?

All the feelings.

Feelings?

Yeah. They're really getting in the way. Besides, you guys promised I wouldn't.

Wouldn't what?

She was really trying to be patient, but they didn't seem to understand. She explained again.

That I wouldn't feel anything. It's really very distracting.

Evangeline, you can't be feeling anything. You know we took care of that. You've had the latest and best adjustments in that area. We've come a long way recently. And you've never had a problem before.

Well, I have one now. It makes it hard to concentrate, and you know you always say that's my big problem.

We don't always say that. It was gently remonstrating.

Well, almost always. When you're not reading me the riot act because I turned left when you wanted right.

She sent it somewhat mutinously; she never had understood why they got so upset that she took a different route, if the destination was the same.

We've been through this before, Evangeline. Now, what is this about feelings? You know you don't have them, except for—

My sense of justice. I know. Then what are all these crazy sensations I've been having? Ever since that first night, everything's been confused.

A quiet rush of air came then, as if they had jointly sighed. *Things tend to be that way around you, you know.*

"Only from up there," she muttered out loud this time. Then, returning to the connection, she tried to explain.

This is different.

How, dear?

Evangeline grimaced. Ever since this patient female had become her contact, she'd felt like she'd been talking to a benevolent maiden aunt. But she was so determinedly optimistic that this mission would succeed without any of the problems of past ones, Evangeline felt guilty every time she did anything that she knew they might not approve of.

It's really strange, she sent at last. The pain was bad enough, but all this—

Oh, my, you haven't gotten involved with that man you sensed, have you? We told you he was off-limits, that you were to stick to Jimmy Sawyer's problem.

I know, but—

No buts, Evangeline.

She couldn't believe they didn't want her to help him.

But he's hurting so much, she sent protestingly.

No. The benevolence was gone, the message stern. *You simply must behave this time.*

The "or else" was implicit. She was walking an even finer line than she'd thought. She wondered if this was her last chance. If she messed up—according to their standards—again, if it really would be all over for her.

She knew then that she didn't dare turn to the bosses for an explanation of what was going wrong. They would no doubt just chalk it up to her lack of discipline again. And maybe they were right. Maybe she had just let that horrible blast of pain unbalance her.

All right, all right. I'll be good, she promised.

And, she added to herself when the connection was broken, I will not waste any more time wondering about Dalton MacKay. He doesn't seem to be in that horrible pain any longer, anyway. Or perhaps he was just managing to hide it behind those formidable walls that were stronger than any she'd ever encountered before.

That doesn't matter, she told herself, echoing the sternness of her boss's command. Jimmy is my mission here, my only mission, and I'm going to concentrate on him from now on.

That decision firmly, solidly and irrevocably made, she climbed into bed, pulled the thick, bright yellow comforter over her shoulders, and settled down to sleep.

And in the morning she told herself she couldn't be held responsible for what she dreamed, even if those dreams involved a lean, dark-haired man who looked at her with eyes so haunted that her heart—which was supposed to be immune—ached for him.

Dalton rubbed at his weary eyes, groaning at the brightness of the sunlight streaming in through the win-

dows across the room. If he had gotten even two hours of
sleep, he'd be surprised. Dawn had been brightening the
sky when he'd at last dropped off. If Mrs. Webster wasn't
bringing in her car—if you could call that behemoth of
hers a car—for an oil change this morning, he'd roll over
and go right back to sleep.

There had been a time when he'd been able to sleep only
in the daylight, but he'd made progress since then. Sometimes he even managed to go a couple of nights in a row
without dreaming. And sometimes as long as a week
without shoving that damned tape into the VCR.

But last night he'd done both. He'd been so restless, felt
so distracted, that he'd known it was coming. And it had
come, the dream, and even more vividly than usual. So
vivid that only the tape, the grim reality, could counteract
it, and he'd spent the darkest hours of the night watching
it, over and over. It never changed, but he kept on, re-
peating it, as if he could somehow etch it into his subconscious and erase the dream. He'd rather dream the horror
than the miracle; waking up to find the horror was the reality was too devastating.

He knew what had rattled him so, even though he didn't
want to admit it. It was that woman, that teacher, the one
Jimmy had brought over. Why couldn't she have been like
that sour-faced, prune-souled woman who was the prin-
cipal, the woman who sniffed disdainfully every time she
saw him, the woman who personified almost every teacher
Dalton had had in his life? But no, Ms. Law—had Jimmy
ever mentioned her first name?—was no more like that
than a go-cart was like an Indy car. And even though
Jimmy had told him she was a looker, he hadn't expected
what had climbed out of that classic Chevy.

A classic beauty, he thought as he rolled over and sat up,
propping his elbows on his knees and cradling his head

wearily in his hands. Although she wasn't, really, he supposed. Her mouth was a little too wide for classic beauty—and too soft and full for his comfort. Her nose was turned up a bit too far—and too sassy for his gloom. Her eyes were too big, too dark—and far too deep and wise for his peace of mind. Too wise for anyone as young as she appeared to be. Those huge, dark brown eyes were almost eerily penetrating, as if she saw much more than anyone thought they were letting be seen.

God, you're tired when you start fantasizing like that, he muttered inwardly. You've got no business thinking about her at all, or any other woman for that matter. You're out of that race, for good, and you'd damned well better remember that.

That's what you get, he lectured himself, for letting that kid get close. You should have kept the walls up. Once you let one person in, they start dragging in others. Well, it wasn't too late. He might have let the kid in, but he could throw him right back out again. So Jimmy's got problems. Don't we all? Let him deal with them. Nobody ever gave a damn about you, and you survived. He'd better learn to survive, too, because nobody was going to help him. And he'd better start learning now.

Dalton stood, rubbing at the scar on his temple, and feeling the ache in his right ankle where more metal than bone held the joint together. He welcomed the pain. It served as a reminder of why he was here, of what he had done. And it was only physical pain, a hell of a lot easier to stand than the other agony, the one that ripped at his insides like the jagged pieces of a race car had once ripped at his flesh.

He strode toward the bathroom, with each step forcing his right foot down harder, heightening the pain. He knew it was the only way to get past it, to work it out. It was also no more than he deserved.

And as he stood beneath the flow of steaming water, he found himself flexing the aching joint fiercely, hoping the ache would be enough to drive the memory of a pair of huge brown eyes out of his mind.

Three

Evangeline smiled at the waitress as she accepted the mug of coffee. The small restaurant was less busy now as patrons hurried off to work, and since her first class wasn't until nine, she decided she would take this chance to speak to the woman.

"You're Mrs. Kirkland, aren't you?"

"Yes." Weary blue eyes sparked with interest as the woman looked at her. "I'm Maggie. You're Ms. Law, the new teacher, aren't you?"

Evangeline nodded. "And I live across the street from you, I think."

"At Lilah's. Yes, I know. I've been meaning to come over and thank you."

"Thank me?"

The woman nodded. "In the two years Jimmy Sawyer has lived with us, he's been trouble from morning to night. Angry, bitter...we can't seem to get through to him at all."

"He is very angry," Evangeline agreed.

"He sneaks out at night, to hang around with those awful friends of his, older kids, real troublemakers. Lord knows what kind of things they're up to. I know they're the ones who set that fire at the high school last year. I think Jimmy was with them, but he didn't get caught. If he had, he could have wound up in juvenile hall."

"He's been through some tough times," Evangeline said carefully.

"Yes, I know that. It's awful, what that child has been through. That's why Bob and I took him on. We have no kids of our own, and we thought...well, we wanted to help. You know, an older child, who probably would never get adopted. But we got more than we bargained for."

A hopeful smile curved the woman's mouth, brightening her weary expression for a moment. "But he hasn't cut class since you came. And the other night he stayed home. He was actually reading a book. For your class, he said."

Evangeline smiled. "I'm glad."

"I've never seen him reading anything that didn't have comics or cars in it."

"Well, there's a lot of wonderful art in comics, you know, and there's nothing wrong with cars. They can be a very healthy hobby, compared to some."

"I suppose," Mrs. Kirkland said. "And I must say, it's been a lot more peaceful at my house since Jimmy started hanging around that garage after school these past few weeks. He doesn't see quite as much of those other boys, thank goodness. I'm not sure about that man, though."

Evangeline went still. "Dalton MacKay?"

"Yes. He's...strange."

"Strange?"

"Oh, not like dangerous, but...unfriendly, I guess."

"I got the impression he was more...detached," Evangeline said neutrally.

Mrs. Kirkland considered that. "Yes, I suppose that fits. I mean, he's lived here for over a year, but he's not really part of the town. And that's odd, in a small place like Three Oaks."

"Yes, I suppose it is. But I imagine he has his reasons."

"My husband says he was famous, a couple of years ago. Some kind of race car driver or something. I don't follow that kind of thing, so I wouldn't know. But I suppose that's why Jimmy's so fascinated with him."

Or perhaps the boy just senses a brother under the skin, Evangeline thought as memories of those painful images came back to her.

"He's a good mechanic though," Mrs. Kirkland said. "He's kept our poor old station wagon going long after the dealer in Santa Barbara said we should buy a new one. And he doesn't gouge us with high prices, either. Barely charges for his labor, just parts. In fact, if he didn't live in that old room over the garage, I don't know how he'd get by."

"He's generous, then."

Maggie looked puzzled for a moment. "Yes, in that way, I suppose you're right. And we're glad to have him, really. That old garage had been empty a long time before he came. It's wonderful not to have to drive twenty miles to have work done, or pay to have your car towed." She smiled slightly. "Mr. MacKay makes house calls. He doesn't even seem to mind, no matter what time it is."

He doesn't care enough about anything to mind.

The instinctive knowledge leapt into her mind fully formed, making her wonder if the bosses had developed some new way of sending information. But they would hardly be sending her anything on Dalton MacKay, so she didn't know where this was coming from.

It wasn't until the woman had gone to serve a late customer that Evangeline realized that once again she'd been diverted, that when she'd meant to find out more about Jimmy, she'd wound up spending almost the entire time talking about Dalton MacKay.

"Jimmy? Can I see you for a minute after class?"

The boy turned red at the chorus of hoots and howls that met her request. But he stayed behind as the rest of the students filed out. They'd had a raucous day; their role-playing as the rebels and Tories of the American Revolution had been lively enough, but when she had stopped the debate and made everyone switch sides, things had nearly gotten out of hand because the two sides knew each other's position well enough to attack with devastating accuracy.

It had taken her nearly the whole class period to get them to see they also knew each other's position well enough to understand each other. In the end, she'd gotten her point across; knowledge was power, however you used it, and neither side was fully right or fully wrong.

"You didn't seem to be with us today, Jimmy," she said after the others had gone, hurrying now that classes were over for the day.

The boy shrugged carelessly. For the past two days— ever since the morning after she'd gone by the garage, in fact—he'd slipped back into his old ways, his attitude bitter, his answers sarcastic and his expression sullen. He was hurting; she didn't need any special powers to see that. He was also tired, yawning throughout the class, and she sensed he was back to sneaking out with his friends at night.

She sat back in her chair, studying him for a moment. "What is it, Jimmy?" she asked gently.

"Nothin'."

She reached out to him. "You're obviously upset—"

"I'm not," he snapped, backing away.

"All right," she said after a moment. Then she stood to gather her things. Jimmy lingered, as if uncertain whether or not he was free to leave. Or as if he wasn't sure he wanted to. As she picked up her jacket, she asked, "Can I give you a ride to the garage? I have to stop at the drugstore on my way home."

His eyes lit up at the thought of a ride in her car, but an instant later the sullen expression was back.

"Nah. I got my bike. Besides, I don't hang around there anymore. It's stupid."

Stupid. It had been the only bright spot in his young life two days ago, but now it was stupid.

"Mr. MacKay will miss you, don't you think?"

Jimmy swore out a negative answer, a crude oath that she sensed came more from pain than the usual teenage desire to shock. "He's the one who threw me out."

Evangeline blinked. Dalton had thrown the boy out? That didn't fit at all with what she'd picked up during that brief but unforgettable contact.

"Jimmy, are you sure?"

He snorted. "He told me to leave him the hell alone. Yeah, I'm sure."

"Maybe he just . . ."

Her voice trailed away as she realized the boy wasn't hearing her. She probed gently, and although his protective walls were substantial—not nearly as tough as Dalton's, however—she finally got it. He'd expected this. To him, everyone in his young life had rejected him sooner or later, his parents by dying, then his grandmother, who had also died shortly after rather dutifully taking him in, and then his other foster homes, by sending him back because he was too much trouble.

And she also got the memory of last night's activities, and had the answer to the graffiti that had appeared overnight on the gymnasium wall.

"I gotta go now, okay?"

It was a measure of respect, she supposed, that he had asked rather than just gone. She had sensed, too, that she was the one remaining light flickering in a world that was rapidly going dark for Jimmy Sawyer.

As the boy walked away, swaggering the moment he got through the door and out where others could see him, Evangeline felt an odd tightening in her midsection. It took her a moment to recognize it, it had been so long. Fear. Astonished, she sank back down in her chair. She was afraid. Afraid she wasn't up to this. Afraid she would let Jimmy down, that she wouldn't be able to turn his life around.

She wasn't supposed to be afraid. Or confused. Or anything else. Even in her disagreements with the bosses she had never been afraid. Nor had she ever been on any of her assignments, even that one with the pilot who had wanted to take himself out and didn't much care if he took his planeload of passengers with him. This kind of work would be near to impossible without an unshakable confidence and utter lack of anxiety. Purposely put in situations of great stress, operatives would be worn out in weeks if they had to go through the ups and downs of normal human emotions.

Nor had she ever doubted that she would succeed in her task, only that she would manage to irritate her bosses in the process. She supposed they had given her that, along with everything else. So why had they apparently taken away that insulation now?

Her hand rose to the pendant at her throat. She hesitated, loathe to subject herself to another lecture on Dalton MacKay. Especially when she'd been behaving herself, staying away from him, and trying very, very hard not to think about him. But how was she supposed to get this job done without thinking about him, when he seemed to be smack in the middle of it? At first she'd thought him an ally, but now that he'd destroyed what little enthusiasm Jimmy had for anything, he was hardly that.

The more she thought about it, the madder she got. In some distant part of her mind she acknowledged that she wasn't supposed to be feeling anger, either, except that which the bosses had finally had to concede went hand in hand with the sense of justice. But that expression on Jimmy's face made her furious at the man who had put it there. Her hand moved away from the pendant and she quickly stood, picked up her books and papers, and strode purposefully out of the classroom.

Dalton heard the rumble of the car long before it pulled into the driveway. He knew who it was; the tap-tap of solid lifters was distinctive. He didn't look up, didn't even move when the car door slammed, just continued to fiddle with the butterfly on the old carburetor that sat in the pan on his workbench.

Swift footsteps approached him. The feminine sound of high heels echoed oddly in the cavernous garage. High heels. He knew he didn't want to look up now; the memory of her legs, exquisitely long and curved, was emblazoned too vividly in his mind. It's your imagination, she's too small to have legs that long, he'd told himself over and over again.

"Just what the hell is your problem?"

It wasn't the opening he'd expected, and his head came up sharply as he looked at her in surprise. And knew immediately he'd been right to be wary; the skirt of her yellow linen suit, which beautifully set off her burnished hair and the golden gleam of that pendant she wore, was shorter than the one she'd worn the other day. Short enough to show shapely knees and tease him with a glimpse of equally shapely thighs.

She wasn't too small, after all, he thought wryly. She was perfect.

Silently he reminded himself of all the time he'd spent trying to chase her out of his mind since her appearance here the other day. Out loud, he asked "Problem?"

"If you want to shut yourself off from the whole world, to hide from everything and everyone, that's your business, but—"

She stopped when he straightened, his face going rigidly still. She'd hit a nerve he'd thought deadened beyond response. He had long ago instinctively sensed that his personal hell took him to the limit of his endurance; the world had to be kept at a distance. He didn't like the fact that she had somehow guessed that.

"Yes," he said, his voice soft, "it is my business."

"I said it was," she went on, her chin coming up as if to show him he couldn't intimidate her despite the fact that, even with her in heels, he towered over her. "If you want to build walls around yourself as high as these hills, fine. I know you have your reasons—"

"You don't know a damn thing about my reasons."

She drew herself up even straighter. There was nothing of the fawn in her eyes now; they were dark and fairly glittering with anger.

"Nor do I care," she snapped. "If you want to hide here and nurse your guilt for the rest of your life, that's fine with me."

Dalton went very still. He'd met this woman once, for all of five minutes, never mind that she'd haunted him ever since. Where the hell had she gotten this idea? Did she know who he'd been, what he'd done? When he spoke, his voice was even softer than before, with an undertone many had once recognized as the prelude to an eruption. He doubted he was capable of that kind of emotion any longer, but this was as close as he'd come in a long time.

"Guilt?"

She looked oddly abashed for an instant, as if caught doing something she shouldn't have.

"Or whatever it is that's eating at you," she said hastily. "I told you, I don't care. But I *do* care about other people getting hurt. You can't let somebody in, just enough to start to care, then slam the door on them!"

To start to care? Dalton's heart slammed in his chest, startling him into wondering if his emotions were as dead as he'd like to believe. Had that five minutes of their first meeting been as indelibly carved into her mind as his? Had she been haunted by it as he had?

Stop it, he ordered himself. Even if she had, it meant nothing. He wouldn't allow it to mean anything.

"He's just a boy, Mr. MacKay. A very troubled boy."

Jimmy, he thought. This was about Jimmy. God, MacKay, you're a fool.

"The last thing he needs," she was saying vehemently, "is the one adult he thought was his friend turning his back on him."

Dalton fought off the twinge her words caused. "I didn't turn my back on him. I'm just not used to having a kid around all the time."

"So tell him you're busy, to come back tomorrow."

"Tomorrow's not going to be any better."

"Nice philosophy. And now you've got Jimmy believing it, too."

"I can't help what he believes."

Her eyes widened. "You don't honestly believe that, do you? He idolizes you! You could make him believe whatever you want."

"Idols," he said flatly, "usually have feet of clay. He might as well learn that early."

She studied him for a long moment. "Did yours?" she asked softly.

Caught off guard by the unexpected question, the answer slipped out before he could stop it, a harsh whisper that was barely audible.

"No."

He backed up a step, unable to bear the gentle understanding in her eyes. That was three times now she'd gotten to him, gotten through to a part of him buried so deep it should have been impossible. It was as if she could read his mind somehow, as if she knew his deepest thoughts, things he rarely dragged out into the light himself.

"Who was he, Dalton?"

His entire body tensed. He wasn't sure if it was because she was treading ground upon which he never let anyone walk, or if it was something much more primitive, much more elemental: the sound of his name in that low, soft voice. The only thing he was certain of was that this had to stop. Now.

"None of your business," he said harshly.

"I see," she said in that same gentle tone, and he had the oddest feeling that it was literally true, that she saw everything, clear down to the twisted, shriveled darkness of his soul. Pressure built up inside him as the threat closed in.

This woman, and the boy she was so valiantly fighting for, could make him lose sight of why he'd come here. He couldn't let that happen.

"Look," he growled, "I don't have time for this. And I don't have time for that damn kid hanging around and asking questions all the time, let alone having him drag in everybody else in town."

It was a moment before understanding dawned in her eyes.

"You mean me, don't you?" Astonishment echoed in her voice. "You're angry at Jimmy because he brought me here? And you're making him pay for my intrusion? Of all the misguided— How dare you?"

He'd known she was angry when she'd first come in, but there was little doubt that now she was furious. He'd never known brown eyes could be icy, but these were.

"You're entitled to wallow in your own misery, Dalton MacKay, but how dare you take it out on a boy who has troubles enough of his own?"

He drew back a little. Not only were those eyes icy, but they had the power to spread that chill; he felt it sweeping over him. And he couldn't think of a damned thing to say.

"If you're mad about my coming here," she said fiercely, her hands on her slim hips as she glared at him, "then take it out on me, not Jimmy! You know what you are? A coward, that's what!"

The chill reached the very core of him then. It numbed all the confused emotions he'd been trying to suppress. He didn't need to rebuild his walls, she'd done it for him. He met her angry gaze levelly.

"Yes," he said emotionlessly. "I am."

He turned away from her and went back to his work on the carburetor as if she were no longer there. There was a long moment of silence before she spoke.

"Dalton," she began, her voice soft and so incredibly gentle he felt as if she'd touched him. He almost shivered under its impact.

"Goodbye, Ms. Law," he snapped.

"Evangeline," she said quietly.

He looked up at that; he couldn't help it. "What?"

"My name is Evangeline."

"Lord," he muttered. "It's bigger than you are."

"And I thought you were a bigger man than you are," she said in that same quiet tone. And without another word, she turned and walked away.

Dalton watched her go, watched her get into the red and white car, fire up the powerful motor, and leave with a bark of rubber that relayed her anger...or her disappointment. He told himself it didn't matter what she thought, in fact, that it was best that she dislike him enough to stay away. She stirred up things, made him think about things he didn't want to think about, saw things she shouldn't have been able to see. She was dangerous, to him and to the carefully constructed world he'd built here.

The more distance between them, the better, he thought. He should be glad that he'd obviously disappointed her so much that she'd never set foot in here again. He *was,* he told himself as he turned his attention back to his work. He was glad.

And disgusted, he added a moment later as he looked down at fingers that were shaking. He slammed the needle-nose pliers down on the workbench and stood staring at his hands for a long time.

This questioning of the objective is highly irregular, Evangeline.

But he's in such misery! You've got to let me help him. *Your job here is—*

Jimmy Sawyer. I know that.

You're interrupting again, dear.

She could tell she was truly testing their patience. She tried to rein in her urgency, but the memory of what she'd felt during that brief but unforgettable contact with Dalton was so strong it was like a spur, prodding her constantly.

I'm sorry. But, really, I've never felt anything like what I get from him.

Remember the primary rules, Evangeline.

I know, I know, no interference in anything that doesn't have a direct bearing on the job I'm here to do. But it *does* have a bearing on it, really. He and Jimmy—

Leave well enough alone, Evangeline.

Her response burst from her incredulously.

Well enough? He's in so much anguish, it's torturing him. It's eating him alive.

A sigh, then, sadly, *We know.*

What?

We know, dear. We know all about Dalton MacKay.

Then you can't leave him like that! That's what this is all about, isn't it? What we do? Straightening things out for people who deserve it?

Yes, but—

You're not saying he doesn't deserve it? I can't believe he did anything to earn the kind of hell he's living in.

You must stop interrupting, dear. No, he hasn't, contrary to what he thinks.

Then I must help him!

Evangeline.

It was a voice of authority, deep and commanding. Uh-oh, she thought. The big boss. She'd really done it now.

Sir?

She wondered if it sounded as squeaky to them as it did in her mind.

Let it be, Evangeline. He does not want our help. He does not want anyone's help. If Dalton MacKay is to survive this abyss he is in, it is up to the man himself.

But...

She stopped, startled at her own temerity. No one, not even she, argued with the big boss. Yet when the booming voice came again, it was oddly gentle and understanding.

Yes, it seems contrary to our purpose. But we have tried and failed. Some things about the human psyche are beyond even our efforts.

They had tried? And failed? She didn't think they ever failed. But if Dalton had been too much for them, then he was certainly too much for her. A feeling oddly like depression settled over her.

Evangeline? It was her contact again. *What is that odd sensation?*

I told you, something's out of whack. I'm feeling things I shouldn't be. Emotions.

But that's—

Impossible. I know. But there it is.

They didn't even comment on her interrupting this time. *Oh, dear. Perhaps you need to come back for an adjustment.*

Not now. Jimmy's in a bad spot right now, and I need to be here.

Very well. But if the problem persists, something will have to be done.

I'll get back to you.

She sat in her room for a long time after the connection was broken, trying to accept what they'd told her. She'd never felt so completely helpless, except in the moments before she had agreed to take on this job in the first place.

At last, when the walls seemed to be closing in on her, she pulled on her jacket and went outside, hoping a walk in the brisk fall air would clear her head.

The streets were dark; most of the businesses in the little town closed early. She wandered past the small city hall and the smaller courthouse, noticing the keystones on both that said they'd been built in 1880. A good year, she thought. Helen Keller was born. Thomas Edison and his electric light. And she'd been in Ohio, in time to hear General Sherman's "War is Hell" speech. She'd thought then that people would remember that phrase, that—

"Hey, honey, come on over here!"

"Yeah, baby, we got somethin' for you!"

The young male voices and the catcalls echoed off the stone of the courthouse wall. Well, *that* certainly distracted her from her worries, she thought. She kept walking, wondering how women who didn't have her options stayed sane.

"Hey! We're talking to you, bitch!"

She stopped, and turned around as the running footsteps approached. Four boys formed a silently threatening semicircle in front of her. These boys would be seeing that courthouse from the inside if they kept this up, she thought.

She recognized three of them as ones pointed out to her by another teacher; the two who had been expelled last year for setting the fire in the school library, and the third the rowdiest boy in the entire junior class.

And the fourth boy, she realized with a sinking heart, was Jimmy.

Four

These must be the friends Mrs. Kirkland had spoken of, Evangeline thought. She could even understand the attraction; being allowed to hang around with older boys had always been a lure to younger ones.

A moment after she recognized Jimmy in the dim light, she saw him do the same.

"Ms. Law!" he exclaimed, startled.

"Hey, she the one I been hearin' about?" one of the older boys asked, tugging on a lock of grimy-looking hair with equally grimy fingers. "The one that's even got little Jimmy here readin' schoolbooks?"

"She's all right," Jimmy protested.

"She's better than all right." The biggest of them stepped forward. A tall, wide-shouldered yet skinny kid, he was dressed in a ripped tank top despite the chill. He looked her up and down, his gaze blatantly lingering on her legs and breasts. "She's *fine*. Built for fun, you know?"

Evangeline stifled a laugh; he'd tried so hard to sound lewd, but the effect was spoiled when his voice cracked. She saw anger flash in his eyes, and was glad she hadn't let the laugh out. This was a boy already far down the path she was trying to save Jimmy from, and she knew the next few minutes could be vital to her mission here.

"So, what are you guys up to?" Her voice was calm. "Besides hassling pedestrians, that is?"

"We haven't even started to hassle you yet, babe," the big one said. His voice didn't crack this time, and a distinct note of menace had come into his demeanor. "We give special treatment to prissy little schoolteachers. They're not so prissy when we're done with them."

Quite suddenly, she'd had enough. A small object lesson was in order, she thought, one that he wouldn't forget the next time he ran into a woman alone.

"Testosterone running a little high tonight, hmm?" she asked blandly. "Careful, you only have so much in one lifetime, you know. Use it all up now, and you'll be an old man who can only think about it."

The big one flushed, and she saw his fists clench. Jimmy and the other two were gaping at her; either wondering when teachers had started to talk like that, or wondering if what she'd said was true.

"You got a smart mouth, *Ms.* Teacher."

"Goes with my brain. You should try to get yours to match some day."

His hands came up then, as if to strike, and out of the corner of her eye Evangeline saw Jimmy move to stop his friend.

"It's all right, Jimmy. Bullies don't scare me."

The big one grabbed her then. Or tried to; he couldn't seem to get a grip. Evangeline stepped away easily, smiling.

"You bitch," the boy muttered, and came at her again.

Her smile never wavering, she shrugged as his hands gripped her arm. Then he was flying through the air. Tumbling, he landed flat on his back in the courthouse flower bed, gasping for breath.

After a shocked moment he scrambled to his feet. He was furious with embarrassment now, and came at her yet again. She held up a hand to halt him. He seemed to slip, almost before she'd even touched him. This time he landed in a rosebush. Complete with thorns. He howled, thrashing around in his effort to free himself, scratching his bare arms.

"I'd suggest you be still," she said as she stood over him. He glared at her, but he stopped flailing. She knelt beside him, still smiling. "If you'd been in any of my classes, you would have learned three very important things by now. One, bullies truly do never prosper for long. Sooner or later they get what's coming to them. Two, never assume you can beat someone just because you might happen to be bigger or stronger. They're very likely to be smarter. And three—" her smile widened "—don't wear a tank top on a cold night."

She stood. The others all gaped at her anew as she held her hand out to the boy who had just attacked her. Warily, looking as if he were trying to resist doing it, he took her hand. She pulled him up easily, despite the fact that he obviously outweighed her by a good seventy pounds. They stood there for a moment, hands still clasped, and the boy's face took on a very strange expression.

"Sorry," he mumbled. "Didn't mean nothin' by it."

"I know, Allen. You won't make this mistake again, will you? You'll remember, the next time you see a woman alone, won't you?"

"Yes," he said, staring at her. "I will."

"Good." She let go of his hand. "You can go now."

"Yes, ma'am."

He and the other two older boys took off running, throwing wary glances back at her over their shoulders. Only Jimmy remained, staring at her.

"What did you do? I've never seen anything like that. You didn't even move, and he went flying."

"Oh," Evangeline said airily, "just a technique some...old friends taught me." Well, she rationalized, they are old. Very old.

The boy shook his head in wonder. "Wow, that was really something."

"It just goes to prove you should never judge somebody by their looks. By the way, thank you for stepping in."

"You didn't need me," he said, still looking a bit awed.

"But it means a great deal to me that you were willing to help."

She smiled at Jimmy, who looked suddenly contrite. "Allen's a jerk," he said.

"He's scared, Jimmy. About life, and what will become of him. He's always in trouble, and he doesn't think he can change, and he's scared about that, too. People who are scared do crazy things sometimes."

Jimmy studied her. "How do you know so much?"

"I listen to people, Jimmy. Sometimes more to what they don't say than what they do."

He looked puzzled. "What they don't say?"

She nodded. "Like Dalton, for instance."

Jimmy's expression changed, turning wooden. Evangeline ignored the change, and went on quietly.

"I don't know why, but in his own way, he's hurting as much as Allen. Or you, Jimmy. Maybe even more."

She thought Jimmy was going to deny hurting, but apparently her statement surprised him too much.

"Dalton? Hurting?"

"Oh, he'd deny it if you asked, but he is. You said it was strange that he came here, when everyone else is leaving, remember? You were right. I think he came here to escape that pain—or to wrap himself in it, I'm not sure which. And he's afraid to let anybody get close to him, for fear he'll be hurt even more."

She saw a flicker of something in Jimmy's eyes, a flash of understanding, of commiseration. And then she saw knowledge join it, and knew the boy had for the first time realized that maybe someone else really could understand how he felt, that he wasn't totally alone.

"Do you think...that's why he made me leave? Because..."

"You were getting close? I think that's exactly why."

Jimmy let out a long breath, and she could almost see him turning it over in his mind. She'd given him enough to think about for the moment, she thought.

"I was on my way for a soda," she said. "Want to join me?" He looked surprised, and she grinned at him. "I hate to drink alone."

Slowly an answering grin, the first genuine one she'd seen from him—other than when he was looking at her car—spread across his face.

"Sure," he said, "if you're buying!"

"I'm a liberated woman," she said generously, and gestured toward the café.

Mrs. Kirkland was working, and Evangeline saw her give a sigh of relief as they walked in; no doubt the woman had been wondering where Jimmy was, and expecting the worst. Evangeline didn't think she'd tell her that up until a few minutes ago, she would have been right.

They took a booth by the window, and Evangeline saw Jimmy grimace as his foster mother headed in their direction. She also sensed the questions brimming in the older woman's mind, and knew that this was not the time. She turned her head to meet the woman's eyes, and concentrated.

Mrs. Kirkland's steps faltered, then stopped. She shook her head, shrugged, then headed back to the counter to say something to the other, younger waitress who was pouring coffee for another customer. The girl nodded, picked up her order pad, and walked toward them. Jimmy breathed a sigh of relief that nearly matched his foster mother's.

"Is she that bad?" Evangeline asked.

Jimmy looked startled, as if surprised she had guessed the source of his tension, then shrugged, accepting.

"Yeah. No. Sometimes." His mouth twisted as if he realized how confused that sounded. "She just gets on my nerves. Always telling me to get a regular haircut, or dress different, that kind of stuff."

Evangeline smiled at him. "It's an occupational hazard of parents, I think."

"She's not my real mother," he said, somewhat fiercely.

"I know," she said gently. "And that makes it harder for you. And her, too. Of course, it would be easy if she just didn't care."

Again he looked faintly surprised, and Evangeline knew he hadn't really ever thought of Mrs. Kirkland's side of things before. While she realized it was natural at his age to think only of how things affected him, it wouldn't hurt for him to be at least a little aware of others, she thought. She gave him a mental nudge, and he glanced over at his foster mother in time to see her sag wearily against the counter, rubbing at her temples. When he turned back, his expression was thoughtful.

It wasn't until they both had large glasses of soda in front of them that she asked casually, "If Allen is such a jerk, why are you friends with him?"

Jimmy lowered his gaze, staring into his glass as he stirred the fizzing soda with his straw. "He's not always a jerk. Just sometimes. Around girls, mostly. Most of the time he's cool." He glanced at her. "You probably wouldn't understand."

"Ahh. A guy thing."

"Yeah. Sort of. Kids pay attention to him, 'cause he's big. And tough."

"Sometimes," she said evenly.

His head came up and, unexpectedly, he grinned. "Yeah. He didn't look so tough sittin' in that rosebush."

She grinned back. "No, he didn't, did he?"

Jimmy slurped at his drink, still smiling. Evangeline felt the skin at the nape of her neck begin to tingle in the moment before a rush of cold air told her the door had opened behind her. She heard footsteps as someone came in, then they halted. She knew without looking, but she turned, anyway.

Dalton stood there, looking at them, his hands on the edges of his battered leather jacket as if he'd been about to take it off. Before she even realized she was doing it, she had let her senses expand, reaching toward him. Again she caught him off guard, and quickly knew that although he hadn't eaten tonight, he was thinking of walking right back out again, certain he wasn't welcome.

"Don't go hungry on our account," she said easily.

She saw him go very still, and lowered her eyes as she chided herself silently for not watching what she said. She'd told herself after that slip she'd made in the garage—letting him see that she knew about the guilt he carried like a leaden burden inside him—that she needed to be more careful around him. Of course, she'd also told herself she needed to avoid being around him at all, yet here she was, the first chance she got, again playing with fire.

When she lifted her gaze again, Dalton was looking at Jimmy. The boy looked back, steadily but silently. Evangeline tested the tension between them; Dalton was trying to think of what to say to the boy, and Jimmy was thinking of what she'd told him about Dalton being afraid.

Finally she felt Dalton give up the battle for the right words and use the only ones he had.

"I'm sorry about the other day, Jimmy."

Jimmy shrugged, as if it meant nothing, but Evangeline knew it had meant everything. Dalton took in a deep breath and went on.

"I was in a rotten mood, but that's no excuse for taking it out on you."

"You mean," Jimmy said slowly, "it wasn't me you were mad at?"

"No. Not you. It was just . . . everything."

"Oh."

There was a world of understanding in the single word; Jimmy Sawyer, Evangeline thought, was someone who understood all about being mad at everything.

Dalton stood there for a moment, looking as awkward as she was certain he felt. Then, miraculously, Jimmy spoke again.

"You wanna sit down?"

Dalton let out a long breath. "Yes." He glanced at her. "That is, if it's all right with ... Evangeline."

Jimmy blinked. "Who?"

"Ms. Law."

"It's fine," she said as Jimmy gaped at her.

"Is that really your name?" he asked as Dalton slid into the seat beside him. Evangeline relaxed; for a moment she'd been afraid he'd sit next to her. But then she realized her relief was premature. Sitting across from him, looking at that ruggedly sculpted face, at those thickly lashed green eyes, was not going to be easy, either.

And it should have been. It should have mattered less than nothing to her where he sat, what he looked like. Lord, maybe they were right, maybe she really did need a readjustment. Something was definitely wrong with her. She was acting very ... human.

"Is it?" Jimmy repeated.

"Yes," she said.

"What do your friends call you?" Jimmy asked. "Angie?"

Her mouth twisted wryly. She never had liked that name, and she'd had more years to dislike it than most people. "Not if they want to stay my friends."

"I don't know, I kind of like it," Dalton said, giving her a steady look that made her nervous.

Great, she thought. Now I'm getting nervous. What next?

The waitress came back, and Dalton ordered a sandwich and a cup of coffee. With the tactics of a guerilla fighter, Jimmy waited until the obviously hungry Dalton had finished half of his meal before he made his request.

"So ... can I come back to the garage tomorrow?"

Evangeline sensed Dalton's split second of hesitation, almost heard him inwardly battle his instinctive rejection.

But it was over so quickly she knew he'd been through it before. And when he answered, although the words came so easily Jimmy never suspected, she knew what the decision had cost him.

"Sure you can."

Jimmy grinned, this hurt, at least, forgotten. "Great."

"After school," Dalton amended warningly, then looked at Evangeline. "Right, Angie?"

The name, spoken in his low, resonant voice, registered, and her eyes widened in surprise. Instead of the usual irritation she felt at hearing that silly nickname she'd hated all her life, she felt a little frisson of heat that raced up her spine and then seemed to spread, enveloping her in a cloak of warmth.

"I know," Dalton said, one corner of his mouth lifting wryly. "You said people who call you that don't stay your friend. But I didn't figure you cared much for me as a friend in the first place, so it seemed safe enough."

She realized what he meant, that he'd made up with Jimmy but that scene at the garage still hung between them. But before she could speak, Jimmy jumped in.

"Safe? Hey, you didn't see her tonight. She tossed Allen Teller on his as—er, backside in a rosebush."

"Did she, now?" Dalton leaned against the back of the booth and studied her for a moment. "I guess I'm lucky you didn't decide to toss me on my backside."

"There's still time," she said, her tone dry.

Then her throat suddenly went just as dry. Something in the way he was looking at her reminded her of how that name had sounded when he'd said it for the first time. She had to fight for the composure that was supposed to be automatic, the calm that was supposed to be effortless.

Jimmy laughed, apparently unaware of the strange undercurrent flowing between them. He began to chatter away like any normal kid on his favorite topic, the dream car he hoped to own someday. Evangeline should have been reveling in this evidence that there was enough innocence left in Jimmy to salvage him, but it was a long, silent moment before Dalton finally turned his attention to the boy. She felt every second of it.

Dalton listened as he finished eating, and occasionally made suggestions and additions—or subtractions—to Jimmy's grand plan. She watched them, with an odd feeling growing inside her. She nearly groaned in exasperation; after all these years, having emotions she could name was bad enough; feeling ones she couldn't even recognize was exhausting.

With his attention on Jimmy, Dalton's guard was slightly lowered, and she knew she could probe deeper. She also knew she shouldn't. He'd been declared off-limits. He didn't want their—or her—help.

She wished she'd asked how long ago they'd tried. Maybe things had changed. Maybe he was ready now. She stifled a sigh; if she asked again, she would only get lectured again. Jimmy, the bosses would say with their tunnel vision, is your only case here.

Of course, if she needed Dalton to help Jimmy, then she would have to use him, wouldn't she? The boy did listen to him. And she'd had to use outsiders to get the job done before, and they'd approved it. So they couldn't argue with it now, could they? And if she happened to be able to help Dalton, too, while helping Jimmy, they couldn't really get mad, right? Satisfied with her rationalization, she probed, ignoring the tiny voice that said she was doing it mainly because she wanted to know more about Dalton MacKay.

She didn't dare touch him, so she reached out and, as if idly, toyed with his empty coffee mug. She knew the traces of his touch would be minimal, but judging from how powerful the images had been after that brief direct contact, it should be enough.

Again, it took her a moment to sort it out. Jimmy had apparently roused all sorts of forgotten memories in this man, memories he'd kept deeply buried for years. She got only bits and pieces, but it was enough to tear at her heart. She saw a big-eyed, dark-haired toddler, barely old enough to understand the cruel older boy who was telling him his mother had thrown him away as a baby, hadn't wanted him and had left him in the trash can in a hospital bathroom. She saw a weeping woman, trying to explain to a child about lost jobs and why they weren't going through with the adoption. And she got fleeting glimpses of a series of homes, some kind, but with too little time for a boy who needed a lot of it, some apathetic, adding to that now older boy's shell of indifference. And one abusive; she had to blink back tears at the sudden image of Dalton, taller and lankier now, staring into a mirror at the bruises that marked his body.

It was these memories that had driven him to break his vow of isolation, that vow she still didn't understand. True, that kind of childhood did little to build trust in others, but there was something much more than a lonely, harsh childhood that had brought Dalton here, like a wounded wolf to its lair, to hole up and either heal or die. Something dreadful, and it was killing him, slowly draining away every bit of his desire to live.

"I told Ms. Law you were a race car driver," Jimmy was saying enthusiastically.

It hit her so suddenly, so fiercely, that for a moment she thought she'd somehow touched him—an image, brilliantly clear, deafeningly loud, astonishingly tactile. She felt cramped in the tiny space, the smell of hot rubber made her nose wrinkle, the roar made her cringe, the sud-

den heat made perspiration break out on her forehead, and
the feel of a jumping, nonresponsive steering wheel in her
hands made her fingers curl tightly in desperation.

She felt a slight thump, then a solid, bone-shaking blow.
The wheel jerked uselessly beneath her hands, out of control. The horrendous squeal of straining tires, the rending
of carbon fiber and the clank of metal giving way echoed
in her ears. Her body tensed, waiting for the crash she
knew was coming.

The image vanished.

She sat there, shaken. Her heart was pounding, her
breath coming in little gasps. If it had gone on another instant, she didn't know what would have happened. She'd
never felt anything like it. Never, even in direct contact
with a person, felt anything so vividly.

"I wish you'd tell me about it. I mean, racing formula
cars. Wow!"

Jimmy's voice was youthful, excited and so normal that
she clung to the sound of it for a moment, trying to get her
bearings. Carbon fiber, she thought inanely. Was that what
race cars were built of these days? She didn't know. But
she'd known in that vision. And suddenly she had another image of that crash, minus the vivid reality this time,
an image that ran, rewound and repeated, time after time
after time, like a film clip caught in an endless loop....

"That's ancient history," Dalton said, the chill in his
voice snapping her back to her surroundings in a way
Jimmy's hadn't quite been able to.

"But—"

"I don't talk about it." Dalton stood, cutting him off
sharply. "Ever."

Jimmy stared up at his idol, trying to mask the hurt.
Evangeline felt trapped, caught between the boy's stunned
pain and Dalton's once again impenetrable barriers. She

watched as he strode away, pausing only at the cash register to pay his bill before he walked out into the night.

"I didn't mean to make him mad," Jimmy said, his voice wavering.

Evangeline dragged her attention back to the matter at hand. "You didn't, Jimmy."

"But I know he doesn't like to talk about that, and I asked him anyway—"

The boy was so upset she knew this called for stronger measures. She reached out and grasped Jimmy's hands; he was so disturbed he didn't pull away.

"I promise you, Jimmy," she intoned steadily, making him meet her eyes, "you have nothing to do with why he's angry. Dalton is carrying around a lot of pain, a lot of grief, and it makes him like a wounded animal. If you probe the wound, he lashes out. It's not your fault."

She sent him all she could of reassurance, and gradually a calmer look came over his face. She let go of his hands.

"Okay?" she asked.

He nodded slowly, looking a little puzzled. "How do you know so much about him?"

She shrugged. "I've seen people like him before, who keep their pain locked up inside. They can't talk about it, to anyone."

Jimmy considered this. "You think...why he's hurting, like you said, is something to do with his racing? That crash, maybe?"

"It does all seem to be tied up together, but I don't know, Jimmy. I don't know what happened back then."

"A guy died."

Evangeline blinked. "What?"

"In that crash. A guy died. Some older guy. He was on the same racing team as Dalton, or owned the team, or something like that. I asked Mr. Kirkland about it, but he's not much of a racing fan, so that's all he knew.''

Was this the answer to Dalton's pain? She pondered that question as she and Jimmy walked up to the cash register so she could pay the bill, and felt a twinge of pain herself when she found Dalton had already paid it.

''You think maybe that's his way of saying he's not really mad? At me, I mean?''

''Probably, Jimmy. It's not easy for him to say it. He's so closed off.''

Jimmy seemed to be considering that thoughtfully as they walked back to the school to pick up his bike, then walked home. He didn't say much, but Evangeline was encouraged. He was thinking deeply and it was hard to stay angry when you were thinking.

At the Kirkland's house, she introduced herself to Mr. Kirkland, a studious, rather bewildered-looking man who was, she sensed, having a difficult time relating to the troubled boy who had come to live with them.

He had apparently gotten a phone call from his wife that Jimmy was in the café and relatively safe for the moment, at least, and he gave her a grateful look as Jimmy said goodbye and ran upstairs. The boy spared barely a nod for his foster father, and Evangeline sensed that he saw the man as vaguely nice but pretty much ineffectual. Which was, she realized as she spoke to the man, just about how Bob Kirkland saw himself when it came to dealing with Jimmy. But she also sensed a core of stiff determination, and thought that one day Jimmy might be surprised at the strength of this man. She sent Mr. Kirkland what reassurance she could, and he smiled at her as she left.

She went across the street and spent a few moments chatting with Mrs. Webster, complimenting her on her lovely crochet work and the old but obviously well-loved pieces that furnished the house, then she went up to her room.

She sat in the comfortable chair, fingering the pendant around her neck idly, not opening the connection, just thinking. Thinking, as she had far too often of late, about Dalton.

She could tell them, she supposed, that if she was going to help Jimmy she needed to know everything she could about the man he idolized. Or that if she was going to help Jimmy, she needed to know enough about Dalton to keep him from unintentionally interfering.

But she knew that the moment she opened communications with them, they were going to know that the qualifier about helping Jimmy was only an excuse. A valid one, perhaps, but still an excuse; she wanted to know all she could about Dalton MacKay for reasons of her own, reasons she didn't fully understand herself.

So how was she going to find out? She'd relied on the bosses for all her information for so long that she was momentarily at a loss. Then she nearly laughed at herself. If he'd been as famous as Jimmy had implied, then he must have been big sports news. So, the first chance she had tomorrow, she would fall back on the classic human way of searching out answers.

She would go to the library.

Evangeline closed the magazine, staring at but not really seeing the colorful but grim cover photograph. Tragedy At Indy, the banner across the photo read. Even the eventual winner of the race had lost out to the coverage of the death of one of racing's most venerated icons. Veteran driver Mick Graham had been beloved by all, it seemed. But he'd been especially close to the young man he'd plucked out of his own support crew and turned into

the hottest new, young driver on the circuit. Dalton
MacKay was going straight to the top, everyone said. And
it was thanks to the mentorship of Mick Graham. A mentorship, the magazine article had said, that had been personal as well as professional; the two had been like father
and son.

Idols usually have feet of clay.
Did yours?
No.

The memory of that exchange, and of the harsh, broken sound of his voice when he'd answered, came back to
her now with stunning clarity. She shivered, wondering
how anyone survived that kind of pain.

She carefully gave the magazine back to the librarian, to
be returned to the stacks—the small Three Oaks library
hadn't quite reached the age of microfilm yet. She wished
it had; she could have done without the grim color pho-
tographs of the spectacular wreck that had wiped out half
the field. It had been a fluke, the reporter had written.
Dalton finding a hole and charging through at the same
instant a tire had blown on the car on his outside, making
it veer sharply. Dalton's car had been sent careening out of
control. He'd broadsided Mick, sending him into the wall.

At the same time she was regretting the grim clarity of
the magazine pictures of the wreck, another photographic
image was seared into her mind; Dalton, lean and fit in his
racing jumpsuit, hair tousled by the wind and a wide grin
on his face as he stood with Mick beside Mick's car during the qualifying runs. He had been, the caption had said,
teasing his race partner, telling the older man he was going to blow his doors off and take the pole position.

She didn't know what had affected her more about that
photograph; the exuberance soon to be felled by tragedy,
the obvious affection between the two men, or simply that

she had never imagined what a happy Dalton would look like. What she did know was that she had to get out of here, quickly. Her eyes were stinging, and no matter how impossible it was supposed to be, she felt like crying.

She'd expected only to learn what had happened, but the story she'd read had told her much more. Not, as she had told Jimmy, by what it had said, but by what it had not. It had not said Dalton was to blame, in fact, had pointed out that he'd been as helpless as Mick once that tire had blown, and that the entire racing community knew there was nothing he could have done. But she knew now the source of that incredible guilt he carried; Dalton MacKay was a much sterner judge than the racing world.

And she knew something else, as well, the identity of the woman he'd been trying to write to that first night, the woman who had caused the thoughts that had swamped him with such a fierce pain that Evangeline had been able to sense it from a block away.

Mick Graham's widow's name was Linda.

Five

"**I** think they were stupid," Jimmy repeated categorically. "The world's not fair, never has been, and never will be."

Evangeline smothered a sigh. She knew where that answer had come from; she'd heard enough like it from Jimmy in the past week, ever since he'd started going to the garage again. He'd made this pronouncement during a class discussion on the Civil War, and at last she felt compelled to confront him about his attitude.

"What," she asked, now that they were alone in the classroom, "makes you say that?"

"You gonna tell me it's not true? That everything is fair?"

"Of course not." How could she, she thought wryly, when the world's frequent lack of fairness and justice was her whole reason for being here? "But neither is everything unfair. No matter what Dalton says."

Jimmy looked at her suspiciously. "How do you know what he says? You haven't been around."

"Maybe I'm wrong," she said, dangling the bait. "What *does* he say?"

The boy hesitated, then lifted a shoulder in a half shrug. "He says if the world was fair, some good people would still be alive."

And some who didn't deserve to be wouldn't.

It came to her so strongly, so clearly, that she knew it had truly been the rest of Dalton's thought, even if he had managed to not say it to Jimmy. She was getting things in the strangest ways on this job. But when she looked at the boy, she sensed he was thinking of something else. With only a little reach, she knew what it was.

"You mean, like your parents?" she asked softly.

Jimmy's face went stubbornly rigid, a heart-wrenching imitation of Dalton's when she had probed too close to the bone.

"Don't matter," he said gruffly. "I can make it on my own. I don't need anybody."

Just like Dalton doesn't need anybody.

This time the unspoken words came from Jimmy, but the sentiment was undoubtedly Dalton's, and her heart ached for both of them. Ached so hard she had to press a hand to her chest in an effort to ease the pain.

She was going to have to see about that adjustment. She couldn't function like this. For the first time she truly began to see the wisdom of the bosses in making certain their people didn't have to deal with this kind of thing. It was impossible. And exhausting. She didn't remember ever living with this kind of tension before.

"That's a very sad and lonely way to live, Jimmy."

He wouldn't look at her. "Dalton's doing okay."

"Is he? Is he really?"

His head came up then. "What do you care? You don't even like him."

Taken aback, the only words Evangeline could think of were the ones she'd used a few moments before. "What makes you say that?"

"He told me so."

She took a deep breath. "Dalton told you I didn't like him?"

"Not exactly. But he said you had a fight."

She reached out with her senses, hoping Dalton hadn't told him what the fight was about. She read nothing of guilt in the boy, as she expected she might if he'd known they'd in essence been fighting over him, and let out a breath of relief.

"We . . . sort of argued."

"He called it a fight," Jimmy insisted. "He said that you didn't like him much, or the way he had to live."

"*Had* to live? Is that what he said?"

Jimmy nodded. "He said you were—"

"Were what?" she prompted when the boy stopped, flushing.

"Nothin'."

"Jimmy—"

"I gotta go. We're going to Mr. Kirkland's mother's tonight."

She could hardly keep him from that, she realized, no matter how much she wanted to know what Dalton had said about her.

"Oh. You'd better go, then."

He grimaced. "Don't know why they make me go with them. I'm nothin' to her, and she's nothin' to me."

"So she doesn't like you?"

His brows lowered slightly. "Why should she like me? I mean, she's always nice and everything, but she kinda has to act that way, 'cause I'm living with her son."

"So you think this lady goes to all the trouble of putting on an act, just for you?"

He blinked, obviously never having thought of it in quite that way. "Well..."

"Go ahead, Jimmy. I don't want you to be late. But think about something for me, will you? You asked why she should like you. Maybe you should look at it this way—why shouldn't she?"

He gave her a considering look as he picked up his books. She thought she had succeeded in planting a small doubt among his assumptions; now she could only hope that it would take root.

And she still didn't know what Dalton had said. As she watched Jimmy hurry away, she almost regretted the restrictions on reading people's thoughts, although she knew they were right, and necessary. Only in case of need, they said, and she knew they didn't mean *her* need.

Her need. God, she thought as she walked out to her car, she missed that cool, calm impartiality she used to have. She couldn't take this much longer. Tonight she would have to contact them, to tell them she needed something done, fast, to get her back to normal. *Her* normal. Maybe tonight, while Jimmy was gone, they could get it done quickly, so she wouldn't lose any time with him.

She was making progress, she could feel it. But every time she got a step ahead with the boy, Dalton MacKay dragged him back. She was sure he didn't mean to, but his outlook was rubbing off on the boy. And that outlook was, no matter how understandable, too sour even for someone Dalton's age, let alone Jimmy's.

She'd been driving for a couple of minutes before she realized where she was headed. She should turn around, she told herself, turn around and go home, contact the bosses, and have them fix whatever it was they had to fix. But she couldn't seem to do it, and when she reached the garage she pulled into the driveway almost against her will.

She wondered ironically if this was how people felt when she exerted her power of will over them to get them to do what she needed them to do at the moment. With a sigh— Lord, she'd been doing a lot of that lately—she parked the Chevy and got out.

Dalton groaned the moment he heard the Chevy pull in. He didn't need this now. He hated doing inventory, any- way—the numbers and paperwork of this business were the worst part—the last thing he needed was to have to cope with Ms. Evangeline Law chewing him out again on top of it. The woman did crazy things to his equilibrium.

I thought you were a bigger man than you are.

Her words, spoken so sadly, had echoed in his mind for hours. And no matter how many times he'd told himself it didn't matter what she thought, that it didn't matter what anyone thought since he already knew the truth about himself, he hadn't been able to forget them.

And who knew what she wanted to yell at him about this time. He'd made sure Jimmy didn't cut classes to come here, and tried to nag the kid into doing his homework while he was here, what the hell else could he do?

He rechecked the card in front of the shelf of oil filters, and made an entry on the reorder form on his clipboard. He went on to the stacks of air filters and made another entry. And tried to ignore those so distinctly feminine footsteps that again were echoing hollowly in the garage as she walked toward him.

She came to a halt. He didn't look at her, just moved to the next stack of boxes.

"I owe you an apology."

He nearly dropped the clipboard as his head snapped around toward her; that was the last thing he'd expected her to say. "What?"

"An apology. I was wrong."

His grip tightened on the pen. He consciously eased it; he'd been breaking a few of them lately. "Wrong?"

"It takes courage for a grown man to apologize to a kid. You're no coward."

"If I wasn't, I wouldn't be here." The words slipped out—as so many seemed to do around her—before he could stop them. He hurried to change the subject. "Congratulate yourself, Ms. Law. You shamed me into it."

She watched him for a long moment, so steadily he almost looked away. But he couldn't, he was fascinated by the way the simple gold knit dress she wore managed to be demure and yet utterly sexy at the same time. It covered her from neck to wrists, and fell well below those shapely knees he remembered so well, yet it clung to every curve as she moved, allowing him to picture perfectly the body beneath. Something he'd been trying to avoid doing ever since she'd slid out of that car and into his mind.

"You know," she went on conversationally, "I never thought I'd say this, but I think I almost like Angie better."

He blinked. "What?"

"Angie. It's much nicer than the stuffy way you say 'Ms. Law.'"

Her tone was too teasing, too friendly, and it would be far too easy to slide into that trap. He couldn't let himself, she'd already dug her way into his thoughts, he couldn't let her go any further. He turned abruptly to face her down.

"How about just Ms. Do-gooder?"

Her brows rose. "You say it like an insult." When he didn't respond, she went on. "Jimmy could be a good kid, Dalton. If I could just get him away from those older kids, the rough ones, and if you could stop telling him how rotten the world is, making him even more bitter—"

"He's got enough to be bitter about on his own. He doesn't need any help from me."

"But he's getting it from you, that attitude. And he's heading for trouble. Those boys he's hanging around with are an awful influence."

"And I'm not much better, right?"

"I didn't say that."

She didn't have to, he thought. It was obvious. "Make up your mind. First you're mad because I sent him away, now you're mad because I'm letting him come around again."

"I'm just worried about Jimmy."

"And you can't let it alone."

She studied him silently. "You don't think I should try to help him?" she asked at last.

He shrugged again. "Help him all you can. The kid sure as hell could use it."

Her eyes went distant somehow, and he had that same eerie feeling he'd had before with her, that she was seeing clear through him.

"And you would know, wouldn't you?" she said softly. "Nobody ever helped you."

He had to stop this. He slapped the clipboard down on the workbench forcefully, and the sharp crack of sound made her start. The distant look left her eyes.

"That," he rasped, "is exactly what I mean. What you do with Jimmy is between you and him. But don't be turning your benevolence on me, lady. I'm not buying."

"No, you're running like hell."

He refused to rise to the bait. "I thought I was wallowing. Make up your mind."

She gave him another of those long, studying looks. When she spoke, her voice was soft, enticing and oddly mesmerizing. "Is this really how you want to live, Dalton? Forever?"

He felt as if he were being drawn toward her, although he knew he hadn't moved. Her gaze was intent now, as intent as it had been unfocused moments before. The strangest sensation filled him, and he heard the slow, whispered words he spoke as if they'd come from someone else.

"The alternative is not living at all. Sometimes I think—"

"No!" He drew back at the sharpness of her voice. He felt groggy, as he had felt trying to wake from a long, alcohol-induced sleep back in his party days.

"No!" she exclaimed again. "Don't ever think that. It's not a solution."

"No," he agreed, still feeling light-headed, only half aware of what he was saying, "it's not. That kind of peace isn't an option."

"Why did you come to Three Oaks, Dalton?" Her voice was soft again, coaxing. He let himself be coaxed, not quite able to remember why he shouldn't. "After all the celebrity, all the big cities, why here, this quiet little place?"

"I...wanted the quiet. So I would...always remember." Was that him talking? He couldn't be sure. "I have to always remember."

"Remember what?"

The safeguards were strong, and he almost remembered why he shouldn't tell her. But her voice was so gentle, so beguiling.

"What I did..."

He felt like he was swaying on his feet, and reached for something to steady himself. Suddenly the mist cleared and he shook his head. What the hell had just happened? It was fuzzy, whatever he'd just said, like a half-remembered dream.

She was looking at him with an expression of compassionate understanding. A look that made him want to run to her for comfort as he'd never run to anyone in his life. A look that made him want to rest, to give up the burden, even if only for a while.

All the things he could never let himself do.

"Just leave it alone," he said, his voice suddenly tight with strain; he had to stop this, stop her. "Jimmy may want your help. I don't."

"I know." Her voice was still soft, gentle, and those urges flooded him again. "You don't want anything from me, do you?"

Every muscle in his body went rigid at the words. What he wanted from her would shock her. What he wanted from her shocked *him*.

What he wanted from her would send her running from him. And since he seemed incapable of running from her, that seemed the only answer.

"Angie," he said, purposely drawling it out. "I knew what I wanted from you the first time I saw you."

Her brows furrowed. "What?"

"You heard me."

"Yes, I did. I meant, what do you want?"

She couldn't be that naive. Not with those ancient eyes. "What any man wants from a woman who looks like you do."

She just waited. "Well?" she said at last.

Dalton stared at her. Her eyes weren't ancient, they were suddenly as ingenuous as a child's. She looked as if she had no idea what he'd been insinuating. He'd never seen such a perfect picture of innocence. Not that his experience ran to innocence, of course. When he'd been racing, he'd gotten used to the groupies, had taken advantage of their presence and willingness. That is, he had until he'd realized he'd meant less than nothing to them; if he had an off year they'd flit away to the next champion, the next new up-and-comer, and never even remember his name.

Even the women who'd come after him after the crash had not been innocents; they'd had their own agenda. They'd seen him as some heroically brooding character who'd just needed a good woman to heal him. It was one of the reasons he'd come here, to this quiet place, to avoid that kind of pursuit. He knew healing wasn't a privilege that would be granted to him; the darkness inside him would never fade. He didn't want it to fade, because then he might start to forget. And he didn't ever want to forget.

"Are you going to tell me what you want, or not?"

"No." It sounded like the growl of her engine idling. "I'm going to show you."

He moved then, that odd lassitude vanished. Before she could react he had her in his arms, and his head lowered quickly. He took her mouth fiercely, hungrily, with all the need he'd been smothering for days now. She went rigid in his grasp, but then, unexpectedly, she softened. He'd meant to scare her, to drive her away, but in the instant she sagged against him, all thought of anything except her lips beneath his and the feel of her body against him fled. Immediately he gentled the kiss, urging instead of demanding, giving as much as taking.

He should pull away, he thought. He should have the moment he realized this wasn't working out the way it was supposed to—she hadn't slapped him and taken off. But he seemed as powerless to stop as he had been to fight that strange fog that had enveloped him.

He was shaking. Shaking. God, he'd only tasted her, gotten just a hint of the sweetness that awaited him; she kissed like an untried girl, primly, her lips together. Yet he was shaking.

He felt her fingers at his nape as she clung to him. He felt the slim shape of her, and slid his hands down her back to pull her close, so close that he knew the picture he'd formed when he'd first seen this dress had been accurate. Achingly, sweetly, hotly accurate. Her hips were taut and curved beneath his fingers, her breasts full and soft against his chest. He could feel the twin nubs of her nipples, already drawn up tight. It was all he could do to keep from moving his hands to those soft curves, to seek out and caress the crests that seemed to be begging for just that.

His body surged in response to the thought, to the hot, vivid images, reminding him with painful suddenness that he had been a long, long time without a woman. At the same time, his mind was telling him he'd never, ever had a woman like this one.

He couldn't stop. He feathered his tongue across her lips, gently, cajolingly. She hesitated, and he did it again, licking, tasting. He heard a tiny moan begin in her throat, and when her lips parted for it to escape, he was ready; he slipped his tongue into the beckoning heat of her mouth.

She filled his senses like nothing he'd ever known before. Like a sunny day in May, when hay filled the air with its scent. Like the sea breeze coming in off the Pacific Ocean, so tangy you could taste it. Like the pure, clean desert air before the race filled the air with noise and fumes.

It hit him then, with a shock that nearly doubled him over. For a moment he'd slipped back to the old habit of comparing everything to the places that had been his life for years—Indianapolis, Long Beach, Phoenix. And he had done it without a single thought of Mick.

Guilt, harsh, corrosive, engulfed him. He didn't deserve this kind of pleasure. Or any other kind.

He wrenched his mouth away and stepped back from her as if she'd suddenly begun to glow red-hot. And when he looked at her slightly dazed eyes, he saw he wasn't far from the truth; the heat of desire glimmered there. She swayed unsteadily, but he didn't dare reach out to her. He didn't dare touch her again.

The heat in her gaze slowly faded, to be replaced with a growing astonishment.

"Oh, my," she said, her fingers stealing up to touch her lips.

"Go home, Angie." He barely got it out.

She stared at him. What the hell was she doing? Why hadn't she taken off running? Why did she just stand there, looking at him as if he'd discovered the cure for cancer or something? He had to get her out of here. This wasn't going at all like he'd planned.

"Angie," he said, putting everything he could manage of threat and warning into his voice.

"I... Couldn't we try that again?"

Oh, God.

"Not unless you want to wind up on your back right here on the floor," he challenged.

He'd meant to shock her; she only looked curious. She glanced downward, as if assessing the floor for comfort. He sucked in his breath.

"Damn it, Angie, get out. I'm on the edge, here."

Her brows furrowed. "The . . . edge?"

He couldn't believe this. No one today was *that* innocent.

"I'm as hard as a torque wrench," he said crudely, "and I haven't had a woman for over a year. Does that make it clear enough for you? Get out, Angie."

"Oh," she said tentatively. Then her brows lifted as her eyes widened. "Oh!"

"Yes, oh."

"Oh, dear."

"That, too. Will you please go?"

"I . . . yes. Yes, I think I'd better."

She gave him a last look, rife with wonder, then turned and practically ran out of the garage. Dalton stared down at the cold, concrete floor and seriously considered banging his head against it until this ache went away.

Six

_____

You have got to do something about this!

Where have you been? We've been waiting to hear from you. Having a free hand does not mean you can dispense with regular reports, Evangeline.

It was odd, how quickly that name had come to sound strange to her, and how Angie seemed to be more who she was. Simply because of the way Dalton said it. The thought made her heart speed up, and she unconsciously clutched the pendant tighter.

Are you there? We can barely read you through all the static. And we got the strangest burst of something on your frequency a while ago. Whatever is wrong? What is all that confusion?

That confusion, she sent angrily, is me!

You? What do you mean?

I told you something was wrong. You've got to fix it. I can't keep going like this.

Calm down, dear. We can see that something is very wrong. All this upset is highly unusual, even for you.

Thank you.

She wondered if sarcasm ever had any effect on them. Probably not; they were always infernally calm. Of course, by normal human standards, she had been unnaturally calm, too. Until lately.

You're still experiencing those feelings?

More than ever.

She hesitated, then decided she owed it to them.

You were right, to numb the capacity for emotion. It's awful.

It seemed necessary, since the nature of the work is so demanding. And living long past the usual human life span would be impossible if one felt an attachment to those ... well, you understand. Besides, human emotions are so ... distracting.

You're telling me. I don't know how people do it.

There was a pause, a silence that somehow managed to seem thoughtful.

Then, *We've sometimes wondered, my dear, if perhaps we didn't recruit you too young. You knew so little of life, and there is only so much we could teach you.*

Thanks. If you'd waited any longer, I would have been dead.

She heard something that sounded decidedly like a sniff. *This new attitude of yours is quite bothersome. You're acting almost human again, Evangeline. Perhaps we truly did take you too young. True, we let you mature a bit before we put you to work, but you were still young in the ways of people. Perhaps that's why you appear to be regressing.*

I don't remember ever feeling like this, even before. So ... muddled.

All humans seem to, at times, so you must have.

I don't think so. At least, not like this. And I *know* I never knew kissing felt like that.

Kissing?

Oops, Angie thought. She hadn't meant to let that out.

Does this have something to do with Dalton MacKay?

She was intensely embarrassed, a feeling increased by the ominously severe tone of the inquiry, and her answer was sharp.

Who did you think? Jimmy?

There was a pause, during which she could have sworn she heard a sighed *Not again,* as if from someone not in on the direct connection. She wondered if they were referring to her muddle, or something else. The thought occurred to her that this might not be the first time things had gone awry for them in the arena of human emotions—it seemed to be their one weak point—but it didn't seem probable to her. They were too good at this, had been at it too long. Besides, she was the one who had the problem predicting human reactions when emotions were running high. That had always been her biggest difficulty.

Evangeline—it came wearily and Angie felt a twinge of guilt; she seemed to wear out her contacts rather easily— *you know this is impossible.*

I know it *should* be. It's never happened before, but...

A sigh—they'd been doing a lot of that lately, too, it seemed—then, *Do you want us to terminate the case?*

Quit? she thought. Just leave?

To her chagrin, the first image that flashed through her mind was Dalton, not as he'd looked tonight, taut with that fierce expression she had belatedly realized was arousal, not as he'd looked the first night she'd seen him, tortured and near to breaking, not even as he'd looked when he was furious with her, ordering her not to turn her do-gooder ways on him. It was Dalton as he'd been in the magazine photograph, young, exhilarated, a bit wild...and happy.

The urge to see him that way again flooded her so powerfully she nearly forgot that she was, in essence, on an open line. She quickly clamped down on the thoughts before they could read them. They'd made it more than clear Dalton MacKay was off-limits, and if she harbored some faint hope that in helping Jimmy she could also help him, it was a hope she'd best keep to herself.

She should be thinking of Jimmy, she told herself sternly. And she was, really. She felt toward him the same need she'd always felt toward the objects of her missions: a compelling desire to make things right.

It was only with Dalton that her circuits went haywire. She wanted to make things right for him, too, but she wasn't at all sure of her motivation. Especially when she looked into those haunted green eyes.

Again she had to cut off the thoughts before they seeped through.

No, she sent. Jimmy needs help. He deserves it. He's had a rough time, and it hasn't been his fault.

And my confusion isn't his fault, either, she added to herself with silent earnestness.

Can you do something? she asked the bosses. That adjustment you were talking about?

Even to herself she sounded somewhat forlorn, as if she weren't quite sure she wanted things to change. But that was ridiculous, she thought. Why on earth would she want to cling to these feelings that had turned her mind into a chaotic jumble? She certainly couldn't *like* feeling this way. And she most certainly wouldn't miss it if they could stop it. Although if they were as curious as they seemed about human emotions, she must be giving them a ton of information.

We've been working on that. We think—

The connection abruptly blanked out. Odd, she thought, and tightened her grip on the pendant. But it wasn't from her end, she realized. It was from theirs. Odder still. Then they were back.

Er, actually, we're ... still working on it. A new procedure. We'll let you know. In the meantime, do the best that you can, dear.

The highly uncharacteristic and obvious evasion startled her so much that she couldn't react, couldn't protest for a moment. Then, just as she pulled herself together, they gave her a rather hasty goodbye and were gone.

What on earth, she wondered, is going on up there? Had they lost control, or what? Was that why she was loosing control, because they were? They were as close to infallible as any beings she'd ever known, but even they admitted they weren't perfect. Of course, that was usually when they were shaking their heads—or whatever their equivalent was—over her and her slightly off-center approach to things.

Well, they'd known what they were getting from the beginning. They'd done enough checking on her to know she never had quite fit in with anybody's plan; her parents, her whole family, in fact her entire world had had an idea of her place that always seemed to be quite different from hers.

But at least she'd had her family for a while, she thought. So had Jimmy, for a few years. Dalton had never had anyone; even the couple who had almost adopted him had tossed him back as if he were nothing more than a bad idea to be given up when things got tough. Jimmy thought he had it rough, and he had, but it could have been worse.

And it would get worse, if he kept on the path he'd begun.

She thought for a moment of those flashes of the past she'd gotten from Dalton. They'd been distressing, even painful, and they were etched in her mind as if truly chiseled in stone.

And maybe, just maybe, it was time Jimmy realized how much worse things could get.

She rose and crossed the room to the only window, which fortunately looked out at the Kirkland residence across the street. They had just been pulling in when she had arrived home, but she'd been far too disturbed—even now her fingers stole once more to her mouth, to touch the lips Dalton had kissed, swearing she could still feel the heat of him—to do more than acknowledge them with a wave. That had been hours ago, she realized in surprise as she stared at the bedside clock. It was after midnight.

She began to probe, to see if Jimmy was home, but stopped when she saw the flamboyant bike propped up near the porch steps; Jimmy was rarely without it. And it was late, and earlier she had picked up the nervousness Jimmy had been feeling when he'd told her about the trip to Bob Kirkland's mother's. She hoped he'd been stressed enough to just stay home tonight and not go out on one of the nighttime prowls his foster mother was so worried about, with those kids Angie sensed would be more than willing to trade bikes for an available car, whether they were old enough to drive or not.

In a few moments she knew she'd been right; Jimmy was there, sleeping restlessly, but sleeping. As she concentrated, setting up the connection, she felt a tug of compassion at the jumbled images, memories of happier times, an older boy and girl grudgingly letting their little brother tag along, mainly because the pretty blonde who had been their mother had ordered them to; of family gatherings and games, and a tall, sandy-haired man tossing his youngest son high in the air with sure hands that would never fumble his precious burden.

And then the picture shattered with a roar and a deafening boom, fire raining from the sky. Jimmy's pulse accelerated and a low moan rose from his throat.

The plane crash, she realized. Swiftly she focused and sent a wave of calmness out to the boy, a vision of serenity, a cool pond in a grassy meadow, shaded by trees and filled with wildflowers and the trill of songbirds. The boy's pulse eased, and she gave him a few minutes of soothing peace. Then she began to send the images, praying that this idea would work.

"I said hand me the five-eighths wrench," Dalton said, his patience strained as Jimmy gave him the wrong size for the second time.

"I did," Jimmy protested, a trace of a whine underlying his voice.

"Then why does it say nine-sixteenths?"

"Well, it looked right." The whine was more definite now.

"Try staying home and sleeping at night, and you might be able to read numbers," Dalton said from beneath the mayor's big, dull brown sedan. He regretted the words the moment he'd said them; the kid probably got enough of that kind of thing at home. "Turn on the air compressor, will you? I'm going to need it in a few minutes to pull these wheels off."

Jimmy looked for a moment as if he were going to argue over the criticism, but when Dalton kept working without saying anything more, the boy went and flipped the switch of the motor that sat atop the drum of the compressor. It came to life with its distinctive chug, and Jimmy walked back and sat on the garage floor next to where Dalton lay on a creeper beneath the raised vehicle, checking the brake lines.

"I *have* been home," Jimmy said after a moment. "At least, last night I was."

"Look, Jimmy, it's none of my business what you do with your time. What is my business is that this place, with all these tools and equipment, is not the place to be if you're too tired to even read the numbers on a wrench." Look who's talking, he added in silent ruefulness.

"Yeah, I guess," Jimmy admitted grudgingly. "But I *was* home last night. Nobody was around to hang out with."

"Why? Allen steal his mom's car and head for the coast again?"

Dalton sensed rather than saw the boy stiffen. The air compressor chugged steadily in the silence.

"How'd you know about that?" Jimmy asked at last.

"I replaced the headlight and the grill he broke, remember?"

"Oh."

The air compressor shut off as it reached the set pressure. Dalton checked the last brake line, then slid out from under the car. He walked over to the air compressor, pulled out the hose, and went to work on the left front wheel. The characteristic high-pitched whir as the air gun loosened the lug nuts made it impossible to talk, and Jimmy watched in silence until Dalton had loosened the last one. Then, as if he couldn't hold it back any longer, he spoke again.

"Aren't you going to tell me Allen's nothing but trouble and I shouldn't be hanging out with him?"

Dalton shrugged. "Nope."

Jimmy looked surprised. "Why?"

Dalton wrested the wheel off and rolled it to one side. "I don't tell people who their friends should be. That's your decision. You have to decide when the potential for trouble outweighs whatever you get out of the friendship." He gave Jimmy a sideways look. "Besides, I'll bet there's some people who'd say the same thing to you about me."

Jimmy studied his hands. "I...Mrs. Kirkland was a little worried at first. But I think she's decided you're okay."

Dalton managed a wry smile. "Should I be flattered, or insulted?"

Jimmy looked up sharply, then saw his expression and seemed to relax. "I'm not sure," he said with a grin. Then, in rather obviously pointed tones, "I think Ms. Law convinced her."

Dalton blinked. Angie? Angie had been talking about him to Mrs. Kirkland? "Convinced her?" he asked carefully.

"She said that you were all right," Jimmy explained. "And Mrs. Kirkland believed her." The boy looked puzzled for a moment. "Everybody believes her, it seems like."

"Yes, it does," Dalton said as he turned back to look at the brakes of the wheel he'd pulled the tire from. He grimaced; this was going to be a bigger job than he'd thought.

"And she always seems to know how you feel, you know?"

"I've noticed," Dalton said dryly. Angie Law's uncanny ability to read his thoughts was not something he wanted to discuss. That she seemed able to do it with everyone didn't do much to calm his unease; she'd struck far too close to the bone for comfort too often, seeming to know what he was feeling before he even knew it himself. It was disconcerting, to have this woman he'd met just a few days ago see so easily past the walls he'd spent years building.

"I told her about that meeting tomorrow, you know, with the social worker? She knew right away I was nervous. She made me promise to stay cool. Made me shake hands on it." Jimmy looked a little bemused. "The minute we shook, I felt a lot better. It was really strange."

He knew exactly what Jimmy meant, Dalton thought. A lot of things were strange around Ms. Evangeline Law.

"Come on," Dalton said. "This is going to take a while, so I'll help you fix that tire on your bike before I pull the rest of the wheels off this crate."

"Okay." Jimmy grimaced. "Don't know what old man Barton needs brakes for, anyway. He never goes over twenty miles an hour."

"The way he drives, would you really want him to?"

Jimmy grinned suddenly. "Good point."

They worked together to get the front tire off Jimmy's bike, and after filling the inner tube with air from the compressor, Dalton told the boy how to find the leak. As he submerged the tire in the bucket of water Dalton had indicated, and watched for the telltale trail of air bubbles, Jimmy said for a third time, "I really was home last night. But I didn't sleep much."

"I know that feeling," Dalton said wryly. "Why?"

"Kept having dreams."

Dalton went still. He knew that feeling, too. Knew it all too well. He didn't want to get into this, it hit too close to home, but the tentative, hesitant tone of Jimmy's voice, as if he half expected to be laughed at, made it impossible not to respond even though the warning bells in the back of his head were starting to ring.

"Nightmares?" he asked quietly.

"Not really. No monsters, or that kind of stuff. Just...weird." Jimmy moved the tube under the water. "Like I was watchin' a movie about myself."

"Yourself?"

"Yeah. Like once I was gettin' arrested. And once I was at a funeral, and nobody else was there. And when I looked in the coffin, it was me. But nobody cared."

Dalton shivered involuntarily at the boy's simple, stark words. He could see why the dream had shaken the boy. It shook *him*. Would anybody care when his time came? Or would they just be glad he was gone, that at last he'd gotten what he'd deserved? The warning bells got louder, but he spoke anyway.

"Sounds like you remember them pretty clearly."

Jimmy nodded as he moved the submerged tube again. "Yeah. Like I said, it was weird, like watchin' a movie. The worst one was—"

Jimmy broke off as a small trail of air bubbles rose through the water from the hole in the inner tube.

"Okay," Dalton said, "pull it out, dry it off a little, and we'll mark the spot. Then you can patch it."

Jimmy nodded and lifted the tube. He let it drip over the bucket while Dalton reached for a rag and a piece of chalk. He wiped off the tube around the hole, still hissing through the remaining film of water, then circled it with the chalk.

As Jimmy went over to the workbench that held the patch kit, Dalton dried his hands and wondered if he should just let the topic of Jimmy's dreams end here. Actually, he admitted with a grim acknowledgment, he was wondering if he could get away with letting it end here. He didn't know how to deal with this, didn't want to deal with it. He was so screwed up himself, he had no business trying to help a screwed-up kid.

The last thing he needs is the one adult he thought was his friend turning his back on him.

Angie's words echoed in his head, and he nearly groaned out loud. Why did she haunt him like this? And why did everything she said have to be right? And seemingly permanently etched into his mind? Damn it, he didn't want to get involved in this boy's problems, he didn't want the distraction. And he sure as hell didn't want the potent distraction of Angie Law, either. He just wanted to get back to that blessed numbness, that day-in, day-out life of boredom, that mechanical, automatic routine that left him time to think of only one thing, the one thing he'd come here, not to forget, but to remember. To always and forever remember. That, through his own arrogance and conceit, he'd killed the only man who had ever given a damn about him.

So let it drop, he told himself decisively. The alarms that had been sounding in his head quieted as the air compressor fired back up again to rebuild the pressure.

He walked over to see if Jimmy was handling the patching all right. He approved the boy's work, and they put the tire back on the wheel. They tested it, found it held, and put the wheel back on the bike.

As he stood watching Jimmy put the chain back on the sprocket, the words came out as if he had never engaged in that mental debate.

"What was the worst dream, Jimmy?"

The boy hesitated, as if he'd been doing some internal debating himself. Dalton didn't push, but realized he was unexpectedly hoping the boy would open up.

"It was... I was in jail. I don't even know what for. But then I saw my mom. She was crying. And my dad. He was just looking at me, real sad, you know? Like ... he was really hurt. He even looked like he was gonna cry. They were there, but not really. Like they were somewhere else, but watching me. What happened to me." Jimmy took a deep breath, and Dalton found himself holding his. "And when I woke up, I couldn't stop thinking that . . . if something like that ever did happen, they'd know. Somehow they'd know. And that's how they'd feel."

For a long moment the steady chug of the compressor was the only sound. Then the motor shut off again. Jimmy shrugged, laughing it off as if it meant nothing, denying the strain that had been in his voice. "Isn't that stupid?"

Dalton wished he'd stuck to the decision he thought he'd made. He should have listened to those instinctive alarms that had always warned him when something threatened his sturdy walls.

He didn't know what to say. But he knew he had to say something, he couldn't leave the boy hanging like that, not after he'd trusted him with something that was obviously discomfiting, painful and very private. God, why hadn't Jimmy told this to Angie? She would know what to say. He wished he had her sensitivity right now, her ability to cut straight to the heart of things.

"Not stupid," he managed at last, somewhat lamely. And then, miraculously, the words were there. "Sometimes dreams are trying to tell you something. Something that your gut already knows, but your head isn't ready to accept yet."

Jimmy considered that. "But . . . these weren't like regular dreams. They were different. So real."

"Maybe because . . ." His voice trailed off. What could he say to reassure the boy, when the vivid reality of his own haunting dream left him so shaken? But once again, as if Angie were there, whispering them in his ear, the words miraculously came. "Maybe the more important the message is, the more real the dream is."

Jimmy seemed to realize then that there was more than just idle speculation to his answer. "Do you . . . have dreams? Like that?"

The alarms erupted again. He could feel himself start to shut down, to withdraw, to back away. *Don't,* his mind screamed. *Don't open any more doors.*

But Jimmy was looking at him, and for the first time Dalton fully saw the scared, lonely boy who hid behind the rough, sometimes rude exterior. He saw himself, scared and confused, and he knew how much Jimmy was daring, what nerve it had taken for the boy who expected nothing but to be slapped down again to risk opening himself like this.

He's more of a man than you are, MacKay.

And for an instant, oddly, in much the same way Jimmy had described seeing his parents, Dalton saw Angie. Looking at him with those huge, too wise eyes, waiting, as if to see what he would do, if he would turn his back on the boy she thought idolized him. It was too much.

"Sometimes," he admitted to Jimmy gruffly.

"About crashing?"

Dalton's gut knotted. God, this was too much, too hard, too painful. He couldn't do it. But then, as unexpectedly as the words had come, the strength came, as if from somewhere outside him.

"No. About not crashing."

Jimmy's brows furrowed in puzzlement. "But—"

Before the boy could get out another word, Dalton felt an odd prickling at the back of his neck. He whirled, and when he saw who was there, he wasn't sure if he was surprised, or if he hadn't, in some subconscious part of his mind, been expecting her.

Angie just stood there, smiling at him as if he had done something wonderful.

Seven

Angie stared at him, delighted but still not quite able to believe what had happened.

It wasn't just the unexpected signal, although that was odd enough, so odd that at first she hadn't realized what it was. As it strengthened, she had recognized it and gasped in shock. Never before had a connection with someone other than the bosses or the object of her mission been so strong. And never had it gone both ways, never had anyone been able to reach her when she wasn't consciously holding the connection open. She hadn't thought it possible.

But there had been no mistaking this. It was Dalton, and he was desperately calling for her help. Oh, not in so many words, she knew that, but he had wished for her, and it had gotten through.

But even more than that was the shock of what was happening in the garage. She had been driving home from school when the signal had come, and she had immediately headed this way, trying for a better image of what was happening. When she'd been close enough to probe, she'd had to restrict it to just sound; driving and the visual images did not mix well.

But even with only sound she'd realized what was happening. Realized, with some joy, that the dreams she'd sent had gotten to Jimmy, rattling him. That he was opening himself up to Dalton. And that, most wonderfully of all, Dalton wasn't running. Oh, he wanted to, she sensed that instantly, but he wasn't doing it. He was sticking with Jimmy, as if he knew that if he didn't, it would be yet another layer added to the boy's protective shell, this time a layer that might never be broken through.

She'd sent him the words, praying that the unusual connection was strong enough in both directions. It had worked; she'd felt both Dalton's relief and Jimmy's tentative acceptance.

And then Dalton had shocked the breath from her lungs when, at the moment that Jimmy dug too deep, the moment when he most wanted to shut down, the moment she felt him nearly turn his back on the boy, he had thought of her. And with her image in his mind he had fought his own need and ripped himself open for Jimmy's sake. She had sent him what she could of strength, but he'd done it on his own.

She couldn't explain the feeling that gave her. She only knew that, as with so many other things on this case, she'd never felt it before. It was a . . . a giddy sort of feeling, she supposed, from what little she remembered of such things. And it was quite enjoyable, not at all something she felt the need—or desire—to be adjusted out of.

"Angie," Dalton said, low and wondering.

That giddy sensation intensified, until Angie wondered if she'd completely lost it and was floating away. "You did wonderfully."

Dalton blinked, and Angie suddenly wasn't certain if she'd said it out loud, or if she had sent it on along that impossible link that had sprung up between them. Her glance flicked to Jimmy, who was smiling at her but not acting as if anything unusual had happened.

She must have sent it, then, she realized. No wonder Dalton had looked bemused. She just *had* to watch herself around him; she seemed to lose track of everything.

"Hi, Ms. Law. We were talking, and didn't hear you pull up. What are you doing here?"

The brightness of Jimmy's tone robbed it of any rudeness. Angie wondered how differently the boy might have sounded had the exchange that had taken place here gone differently. Or if he would even still be here at all.

She looked at Dalton again. And then, on a wave of sensation, she got an image from his mind—of her in his arms, his mouth on hers, building, expanding heat between them. It nearly swamped her, and she sucked in her breath. She was suddenly very aware of the soft, swirling dress she wore, because Dalton was looking at the buttons that ran down the front as if he wanted to undo them. This could be dangerous, this unexpected connection.

Jimmy's look changed from inquiry to curiosity, and she realized she had never answered him. And that she was, to his eyes no doubt, acting rather strangely.

"Er," she began hastily, "car trouble."

She felt Dalton relax a little, and knew he'd been wondering how she'd managed to show up just after she'd been so vividly in his mind.

"With the '57?" Jimmy asked.

She nodded, wishing she'd come up with something else.

Dalton, recovered now, glanced from her to the car and then back. "What's wrong?"

Darn, Angie thought. He knew the car had been fine just the other day. "Ah . . . a spark plug wire, maybe?"

"The motor's missing?"

She nodded. "I was...close, so I thought I'd stop in and see if you had time to look at it."

He nodded. "Pull it on in," he said, indicating the repair bay next to the sedan he'd been working on.

She turned to do as he said, then stopped. She glanced at Jimmy, then back at Dalton. She thought about sending the idea to him, but before she could even begin, he nodded at her. She looked back at Jimmy.

"Want to do it?"

Jimmy gaped at her. "For real?"

"If it's all right with Mr. MacKay. It is on his property, after all."

Jimmy spun around to face him. "Dalton? Can I? Please?"

Dalton lifted one shoulder casually, as if he had all the confidence in the world in Jimmy's capabilities. "Sure. Just don't ding it, or Ms. Law may flunk you."

"Aw, she wouldn't do that. She's fair."

Apparently totally unconcerned with his sudden lack of "cool," Jimmy scampered toward the Chevy. Dalton watched him go, then looked at Angie.

"Quite a testimonial."

"From Jimmy," she said, "that was a fanfare of trumpets."

"Especially since I've got him convinced nothing in the whole world is fair?"

"I think," she said slowly, "that you could unconvince him as easily as you convinced him."

He gave her a look that told her he still didn't believe he had that much influence, but said only, "And you think I should?"

"I think there's a middle ground somewhere, Dalton. Life isn't always fair, but it isn't always awful, either."

She felt the coming rejection of that idea, but before he could voice it Jimmy was guiding the Chevy into the repair bay with exquisite care. Angie watched, to make sure all went well, but Jimmy didn't need her help. He pulled up until Dalton signaled him to stop.

"Leave it on," Dalton told him.

Jimmy nodded, and slid out of the driver's seat with an excited little whoop.

"It sounds okay to me," Jimmy said, listening.

Oops, Angie thought. She'd been paying too much attention to Dalton and not enough to the matter at hand. She'd better do something about this problem she'd made up.

"Sometimes these things are intermittent," Dalton was saying as he walked to the front of the car.

As he lifted the hood, Angie quickly sent a little pulse of energy toward the car. It didn't quite work so she did it again, and this time felt the response she wanted. A split second later, the motor hiccupped obligingly. And kept hiccupping. She let out a breath and relaxed.

"Is that it?" Jimmy asked.

Dalton nodded as he bent over the fender and reached into the engine compartment, his hands moving competently. Angie watched him, only vaguely aware of Jimmy running around to watch from the front of the car.

"Why do you leave it running?" Jimmy asked.

"To check the plug wires."

"How?"

Dalton flicked a glance at Jimmy, and Angie remembered what he'd said about not being used to having a kid around all the time. He wasn't used to having to explain every step of what he was doing to an eager, full-of-questions kid.

"You pull each one loose, and if the engine starts running rougher—" he tugged a wire loose and a moment later the motor shuddered "—like that, you know it's good. If there's no change, then you know you've got the one that's already bad."

He really was being patient, she thought as Jimmy continued his barrage of questions. He really wasn't used to kids, or anyone else being around him, yet he was making a tremendous effort for Jimmy. And somewhere, deep in her heart, she cherished the thought that this might be the impetus he needed to rejoin the world, that in reaching out to help Jimmy, he might find there was still something worth living for—really living, not this cloistered existence—in his own life.

She studied him as he worked. He really was quite good-looking, she mused. She liked the way his hair fell over his forehead, and the way the length of it brushed his shoulders. She liked the strength of his jaw, and the straight, even shape of his nose. And those eyelashes...

If he had been her mission, what would she have done? she wondered. Simply dragged him kicking and screaming back into life? Or, as she had with so many others, simply presented him with the irresistible lure, the woman he'd been meant for?

Something sharp, clawed and unbearably hot tore at her. She nearly doubled over, and sucked in a quick, deep breath to try to ease the pain. Her hand shot to the pendant, but she knew she couldn't send up a call for help here, in front of both of them.

After a moment the pain faded. She made herself focus on Jimmy, who was still rattling off questions.

"Then what? What do you do when you find the bad one?"

"You check the connection. Then test the plug itself, and make sure it's good. Then you test the wire, at both ends."

"Why?"

Angie sensed Dalton again reining in his impatience, but when he answered the boy, it was evenly enough. "It can be broken inside the insulation where you can't see it. Then you have to replace it."

It was curious, she thought. With all the men she'd dealt with over the years, sometimes on a mission to help them, sometimes to help their destined mate, some of them had been strikingly handsome, some of them simply with good, loving hearts that glowed beyond any physical attributes, but never once had any of them made her feel like this one did. She was aware of male beauty, but never once had she caught herself reacting like this to a male face, a mane of hair, or to the way jeans could hug a taut, high backside—

Oh, God. She cut her own rambunctious thoughts off sharply. What was she thinking? What on earth was happening to her? Was this how they had felt, the women she'd helped over the years, the ones who had found the mate they'd been destined for? Was this what she'd never understood, that indefinable attraction that she'd known existed but had always watched with a sense of almost smug indulgence?

Pay attention, she snapped silently at herself. She watched as Dalton tugged on a wire and it gave, but no change came in the motor's sound.

"That's it," Dalton said with satisfaction. He glanced at her, a look that seemed equal parts approbation and speculation. "Good call, Angie."

Her heart seemed to take that crazy tumble again. She tried to steady herself as Jimmy clambered up on the bumper to peer at the motor.

"You found it?"

"Yep. This wire was loose."

"So now you try and put it back in right first, right?"

This time Dalton managed a smile for the boy. "Right." Angie saw him start to reseat the wire she'd loosened, then he stopped. He looked at Jimmy, hesitated, then said in a rush, "Here." He indicated the wire. "Why don't you do it?"

"Me?" Jimmy's voice squeaked with astonishment. Angie wanted to hug Dalton for doing this, for seeing the need in the boy and responding to it.

"Just take the wire here—" he showed the boy where to hold it "—and see that little boot connection? Just make sure it's in solid."

Jimmy's fingers were shaking, but he took the wire. It took him three nervous tries, but he finally got it right. And the motor, cooperatively, smoothed out.

When Jimmy yelped with delight, jumping down from the bumper and turning to Angie, when she saw the pride and happiness in his face as he exclaimed, "I fixed it for you!" she didn't want to hug Dalton. She wanted to kiss him. Hard and hot, like he'd kissed her.

Dalton had been washing his hands, but at the instant that thought flashed into her mind, his head came up sharply. He stared at her, and she saw his lips part as he took in a quick, short breath.

God, had she sent it to him? Had the image that had leapt to vivid life in her mind somehow traversed that odd connection between them? She felt color rise in her cheeks, and it heightened as she remembered the wish that had come next. That this time, he wouldn't stop the kiss.

Please, she begged, she wasn't sure of whom, he hadn't gotten that, had he?

"Did you hear it, Ms. Law?" Jimmy crowed. "It smoothed right out."

"I...heard, Jimmy. Thank you."

"I did good, didn't I, Dalton?"

"Yes." His voice was taut, strained. "You did good, Jimmy."

"Can I do some more things, easy things like that?"

"Maybe." Dalton answered the boy, but his gaze was fastened on Angie. "Later, though. I'm through for to-night."

"Oh." The boy sounded downcast, but seemed to take heart from Dalton's semi-promise of later.

"You'd better get going, Jimmy. I have to talk to Ms. Law anyway. Close that door as you leave, okay?"

There was something very odd in his voice, and it made Angie's breath catch in her throat. Jimmy's forehead creased, then cleared.

"Oh, the bill, huh? Okay. I hate that paperwork stuff."

Spoken exactly like Dalton, she thought. She managed a cheerful enough wave as the boy went and picked up his bike, but nearly jumped as, instead of the door to her car that she'd assumed Dalton had meant, he hit the control for the big, heavy, roll-up garage door. She saw the boy look back at Dalton and wink as he rode off, and she knew he'd done it intentionally. It wasn't hard to guess what the boy had in mind.

The big door rumbled down noisily, and the combination of the knowledge that she would soon be closed in here with Dalton, and the memory of that undertone in his voice, made her very edgy. She walked over to the open car door, wondering how to phrase her request that he raise the big door again so she could get out of here. Dalton followed her, and stood so closely behind her that, although it took most of her nerve, she had to turn around and look at him.

He met and held her gaze, until she wanted nothing more than to look away from the intensity of it. At last he spoke, very, very softly.

"What's going on, Angie? What is it that happens between us?"

"I..."

He lifted his hands to the roof of the Chevy and the top of the driver's door, capturing her neatly. "Don't say you don't know what I mean. You can't not feel it. At first I thought you were just very perceptive. Enough to guess what I was thinking. Maybe I even thought it was ESP or something, even though I think that stuff is a crock. But how do you explain it going the other way?"

She tried to stall. "The other way?"

His hands came up to grip her shoulders. "Don't lie, Angie. Just explain how I knew exactly what you were thinking a moment ago."

She felt that heat rise in her cheeks again as the memory of his kiss leapt to life in her mind once more. His fingers tightened.

"Exactly," he said flatly. And too late she realized that she had just proven his words true.

"I don't know," she said honestly and a bit desperately.

"So I was right. And the words, did those come from you, too? They must have. I never know what the hell to say at times like that. But I thought of you, and there they were. It was even as if it was your voice, saying them, in my head."

"Dalton, I don't know what's happening—"

"Well, neither do I," he said. Then, pointedly, "But I promise you, the next time I kiss you, I *won't* stop."

"Oh, God," Angie moaned.

"I swore when I came here that the sexual part of my life was over. For good. And I've held to it, Angie. It's been easy, because I haven't given a damn. I haven't felt a thing for any woman. Hell, I haven't even been horny."

The word made her blush deepen. But she understood him; he'd cut himself off so thoroughly from any human contact—for some reason she still didn't completely understand, some reason based in the unreasoning guilt he carried—that he hadn't allowed himself to feel even the most basic of needs. As if he felt he didn't deserve even the most fleeting of pleasures.

"But this," he said, his voice going even lower, harsher, "this is crazy. This is more than I can deal with. I don't know what you're doing to me, but—"

"I'm not doing anything," she protested, feeling doubly helpless because it was true. She wasn't, at least not intentionally, doing anything.

"Then what is this? What the hell is happening? Why can't I get you out of my head? Why is it whenever I see you, I forget all the vows I've made to myself? Why is it all I can think of is wanting you, wanting to take you and you to take me again and again until we both fall asleep with me still inside you because we're too exhausted to move?"

She paled as if he'd slapped her. She knew how human sexuality worked, she knew the mechanics . . . but she had never heard stark, raging need expressed so vividly before. And never had it ever been directed at her.

As she stared at him, a change came slowly over his face. Heat and angry confusion was replaced by something else, chagrin and an odd tenderness that she couldn't quite describe and that was utterly unexpected. Tenderness and Dalton MacKay seemed incompatible. Until now.

"How do you do that?" he asked, shaking his head in bewilderment. "How can you be so wise, so complicated and yet so innocent? How can you give me a look that could melt steel, then be so shocked when I put that look into words? Is this some kind of game?"

"No," she whispered, the loudest voice she could manage. "I swear, Dalton, this is no game."

"Then what—"

"I don't know. I swear, Dalton, I don't know. I don't know what's wrong with me. I only know this shouldn't be happening."

He drew back a little. "Wrong with you?"

Oh, Lord, she was messing this up. Just as it seemed she screwed up everything. Maybe they were right, and it didn't really matter that everything seemed to come out right in the end, not when she messed up so much in the middle.

"I mean . . . this has never happened before."

"Believe me," Dalton said grimly. "Nothing like this has ever happened to me before, either."

She didn't know what to say, was afraid to say anything at all, afraid it might make things worse. So she just looked at him, knowing all her confusion must show in her face.

"Ah, damn it, Angie," Dalton said at last, lifting a hand to run the backs of his fingers over her cheek.

At his touch a wild, sudden longing filled her, a longing she couldn't name because she'd never known it before. It was all tangled up with her confusion, all the unaccustomed emotions she'd been experiencing, and his response to her. And it seemed to have been inflamed by that gentle touch.

Dalton froze, his fingers now beneath her chin. His eyes darkened, and she heard him take in a quick breath. Too late she realized that this, too, was showing in her face.

"God," he said on a long, soft exhalation. "Don't look at me like that."

"Oh, Dalton, I . . ."

Her voice trailed away. There were no words to say in the face of the look that came into his eyes then; it was hot and urgent, yet still with that touch of unexpected tenderness. It weakened her body and clouded her brain, until she could barely remember anymore why this was impossible, why it couldn't be.

She tried. She truly did. Her hand crept up to the pendant, her spinning mind clinging to her one last chance. She would make them pull her out, right now, and figure out a way to explain it later. She would just make them do now what they would be doing later, that is, erasing all traces of her time here from everyone's mind. Then Dalton would never even wonder what had happened to her, because he wouldn't even remember she existed. And if that hurt her more than anything had in the last century or so, it was her own fault; at least Dalton wouldn't remember.

But she would remember. She would always, always remember. With a shiver, her fingers curled around the pendant.

They weren't there.

It wasn't just that they weren't answering. They weren't there. For whatever reason, they had shut down the channel altogether. She couldn't even send the message to signal them to call her back. They had at last, apparently, abandoned her. She was alone.

No, not quite alone. Dalton was here. He was here, he was gazing at her with that look, and his fingers were gently stroking her chin, her cheeks, her nose, her lips. He was here, and in this moment he seemed more powerful to her than the bosses ever had. For all their wisdom, all their wondrous powers and technology, they had never been able to give her one basic necessity, because they lacked it themselves. Even they didn't completely understand the workings of love.

But Dalton could show her everything she'd never understood.

"Angie," he said again, a mere breath of sound.

In that instant, as his whisper of her name sent that almost familiar frisson down her spine, Angie made one of the decisions she had become infamous for.

"Yes," she murmured.

Dalton went very still.

"Please, Dalton." She tried to concentrate, but his fingers were still at her lips, and she was having difficulty thinking of anything except that she wished he would replace them with his lips. "I need to understand. I know it's why I get in such a muddle sometimes, because I've never really understood what all the fuss was about."

It was true, she thought. She just didn't know. It wasn't her fault. Even the bosses seemed to agree now, with all their talk of having recruited her too young.

Dalton was looking at her, the heat in his eyes touched with confusion, and she realized how strange her words must have sounded to him. And she also realized that she would have to be careful, on guard with her thoughts because of this strange connection that had sprung up between them. But none of that changed her mind.

"Teach me, Dalton. I want to learn."

He groaned, low and deep in his throat. Then he pulled her into his arms.

Eight

She'd heard all the phrases. Falling in love. Swept off your feet. The heat of passion. Logically, she'd understood the words. She'd seen them in action. She'd even, on cases, sometimes made sure they happened. But never had she ever truly known what they meant. Until now.

The moment Dalton's mouth came down on hers she knew. She knew that this was something bigger, more powerful than anything she'd ever dealt with before. She knew that she was about to learn what she'd longed to know for so very long. At last she would understand.

And then she didn't know anything except the rising, expanding heat that radiated through her with a speed that took her breath away.

When she felt him probe her lips with his tongue she parted for him without thinking. She remembered so vividly the hot, male taste of him, the intimacy of his invasion of her mouth. Knowing what was to come did nothing to lessen the impact; when his tongue brushed hers, she felt fire leap along her nerves.

Barely aware of what she was doing, she reached up and slid her hands around his neck, her fingers sliding through the thick, dark silk of his hair. She could feel his heat, warming her, yet it was nothing compared to the heat burgeoning inside her. A heat unlike anything she'd ever known, a heat that caused an urgency in her, an urgency she didn't understand, a striving for something she couldn't name.

She only knew that he held the answer, and that she had to get closer to find it. He was so tall, so big and solid, that she had to stretch to do it. She pressed herself against him, thrilling to the rough sound that rose from deep in his chest as she moved. He began to move then, his hands sliding up and down her back, his mouth devouring hers as if he were starved for her taste.

She could hardly believe that the low moan she heard was coming from her. She sounded so... needy, as if even the deepness of this kiss wasn't enough. Then Dalton's hands moved again, slipping down to her hips, and he pulled her hard against him.

Even that wasn't enough, and she twisted against him, trying to get closer still. She heard him suck in his breath, then let it out in a harsh groan. Only then did she realize the significance of what she'd been feeling, the meaning of that rigid column of flesh that was pressed against her belly. Tentatively she shifted her hips, using her body to caress him.

He growled something she couldn't understand, muffled by her own mouth. Then he broke the kiss. He drew his head back, but made no move to release her body. His breath was coming in deep pants, and she understood why; the cavernous garage was suddenly short on air.

He simply stared at her for a long moment. Silence spun out between them, but Angie could see by the clenching of the muscles along his jaw, by the tightening of his lips, that he was trying to regain control. And if he did, she knew, he would leave her. She felt suddenly bereft.

"You promised you wouldn't stop," she said, not even caring that she sounded like a mournful child.

Dalton groaned again. "God, Angie, don't. Don't look like that. Don't sound like that."

"But you said—"

"I said too damn much. I always seem to, around you."

She looked up at him, her eyes wide with puzzlement. "You...don't want to, now?"

He laughed, a short, harsh, rasping sound. "I don't want any of this. You're making me feel, lady, and I don't like it." Then he moved his hips sharply, nudging her with his swollen flesh. "But I don't seem to have much choice. I want to, all right. But if we don't slow down, it's liable to be right now, right here in the back seat of your damned car."

Angie blinked. She had, over the years, seen people make love in far more bizarre places than this. In fact, cars seemed to be quite popular. But perhaps Dalton didn't like the idea. "Is that...wrong?"

She heard his breath catch. "Lady, you turn those big brown eyes on me and nothing seems wrong. But I'm not prepared for this."

Involuntarily, her gaze slipped downward, to the obvious bulge straining at the worn denim of his jeans. Admittedly she didn't know much, but he certainly *seemed* ready.

With an odd, choking sound, Dalton grabbed her hand and dragged it down between their bodies until her palm rested against his zipper, over the place she'd been looking at. Instinctively her fingers moved, tracing his erect length, stroking as her eyes widened in wonder at the size and heat of him.

"That," he said tightly as her fingers moved over him, "is not the kind of prepared I meant. I meant prepared to keep you from getting pregnant."

"Pregnant? Me?" Angie blinked again, startled into stillness. "I can't."

"You're sure?"

She nodded. The bosses had made certain of that, just in case, although with the powers they'd given her it was unlikely she'd ever run the risk of being raped. Of course, if the bosses had truly deserted her....

She didn't care. She wanted this. She needed this. She needed Dalton.

She resumed her caresses, and this time he released her hand, giving her the freedom to do as she would. He shifted his body to make it easier for her to touch him, and his hands slid up to cup her head, his fingers threading through her hair as he tilted her head back for another kiss. Another searing, piercing, mind-clouding kiss.

No wonder people couldn't think rationally at times like this, Angie thought dizzily. No one could think at all, feeling like this. On that realization she gave up the effort, surrendering to the rising wave of luxurious heat and the thrill of feeling and hearing Dalton's response as she continued to stroke him.

She only realized when she felt cooler air on her skin that he had unbuttoned her dress. She felt a qualm as he moved to cup her breasts, but the moment she looked down at his strong, work-roughened hands against her soft, pale flesh, it vanished in a new wave of sensation. Then his thumbs crept up to fondle her nipples, bringing them to taut, exquisitely sensitive peaks, and she cried out in amazed wonder.

When he moved to unfasten her bra, she felt no qualm at all, only a growing need to feel his touch on her naked flesh. When the lacy fabric fell away, instead of moving to cover herself, she found herself arching her back, thrusting her breasts upward, shamelessly begging for skin against skin.

He obliged her with a smothered groan, his hands moving, his fingers tightening around the tips of her breasts just enough to make her gasp at the pleasure it gave her. Then he was plucking at that aroused flesh until it darkened to deep rose beneath his touch, and she moaned as her nipples contracted into pebble-hard nubs that seemed to beg for even more. Although what more there was she couldn't imagine.

And then he showed her, moving swiftly to take one tight little crest into his mouth and suckle deeply. The shock of his wet heat made her cry out as fire swept through her, seeming to flare and then condense into a hot, pulsing glow somewhere low and deep inside her.

His tongue flicked at her, and she arched again, convulsively. He moved to her other breast and repeated the caress, and Angie heard her broken little moans begin to run together into one continuous sound of whimpering pleasure.

Her fingers trembled as she tugged at his shirt. She thought, in some tiny part of her mind that hadn't already been turned to cinders by his passionate heat, that she should be able to do this by merely thinking it done. But she couldn't focus her powers, not when he was drawing her nipple so deeply into his mouth, not when she could feel every tug of his lips and tongue in that place of pooling, growing flame. It was all she could do to keep the mental wall between them intact; she sensed he would not welcome the opening of that link just now, and she wasn't sure she could deal with it herself.

She kept fumbling with his buttons. When he realized what she was trying to do, Dalton helped her. He yanked away his shirt without ever taking his mouth from her; she vaguely heard the dance of popped buttons across the garage floor.

The sensation that spiraled through her when she first smoothed her hands over the bare, sleek skin of his chest was as powerful as what she'd felt when he'd touched her. It was something she hadn't expected—yet another thing she hadn't understood—that touching the other person was as thrilling, as arousing, as being touched. The generosity she'd seen in true lovers was so much more fathomable to her now....

And that was the last rational thought she had. Dalton had finished unbuttoning her dress and it fell away from her body. He froze for an instant, staring.

"Oh, God. Stockings. You're wearing stockings."

She felt herself color. "I . . . don't like panty hose."

The truth was, she'd never gotten used to them. Other items of newer, fancy lingerie—although some of it was entirely too racy for her modest tastes—certainly appealed to her after a young womanhood spent in corsets. But panty hose had always made her feel too constricted. So stockings and garters it was, and she was much more comfortable that way.

She'd had no idea it was to such masculine taste, as well. But she couldn't deny the flare in Dalton's eyes in the moment before he closed them, as if the sight of her was too much for him to bear.

"Dalton?" she whispered.

"Just...give me a minute." His voice was thick, rough.

"Is something wrong?"

"Just that...it's been a long time, Ange. If I don't slow down now, I might hurt you."

"Oh, no. You couldn't do that."

His only answer was a low sound of fierce intensity. She didn't want him to slow down, she thought. She wanted to understand. She wanted to know. She wanted Dalton to teach her. She wanted Dalton period. And she wanted him now. He might have been waiting over a year, but she'd been waiting a very, very long lifetime.

She wrapped her arms around his shoulders and lifted herself up until her breasts, nipples still wet from his mouth, rubbed temptingly against his chest. She felt him tremble as if a convulsion had swept through him, rippling through every muscle in succession.

"Don't wait, Dalton," she whispered. "And don't go slow."

A low, growling sound ripped from his throat. He exploded into movement, picking her up in strong arms in the same instant as he shoved the driver's side of the front seat of the Chevy forward out of the way. He deposited her in back, every muscle straining to do it carefully and slowly enough not to hurt her. He pressed her back on the seat, dragging her silk panties down her stocking-clad legs with one hand while the other fumbled with his belt buckle and then the snap of his jeans.

She moved to help him, lingering for another long, slow stroking of the ridge of flesh behind it before she reached for the tab of his zipper and pulled it down. As if that final caress had pushed him past the limits of his restraint, he took her helpful hand and put it around his waist, then shoved away interfering cloth. With his knees, he pushed her thighs apart. For an instant he stared down at her. And in a voice that sounded like velvet spread over gravel, he gave her a last chance to change her mind.

"Angie . . . you want this?"

"I want *you*," she corrected, a little breathlessly. "And I'm tired of waiting."

With a low groan, he moved swiftly, lowering himself to her and into her in one smooth thrust.

Angie had known it would hurt, had prepared herself for it, but she hadn't dared—and hadn't wanted to—invoke her ability to make it not hurt, for fear it would open the channel between them. Her breath caught on a little cry of pain.

Dalton froze, then moaned under his breath. "Damn, Ange, why didn't you tell me? I can't stop now."

"Don't you dare stop."

Her voice was full of awe. She'd expected the pain, but she had never expected, hadn't known enough to expect this incredible fullness, the wonderful feeling of having his body inside hers. She'd of course known a woman had the capacity to take a man, but she'd never realized how exquisitely tight the fit could be, how utterly intimate the process was.

With a strangled-sounding apology that she hushed, Dalton began to move. His hips rocked against hers, driving him even deeper, then drawing back. She heard herself whimper at his withdrawal, but it coalesced into a throaty sound of pleasure as he filled her again, and again. She moaned at the sweet rhythm, marveled at the luscious friction, and cried out at the wonderful fullness as he buried himself in her to the hilt.

He murmured her name, low and rough, and began to move faster. Something about his increased pace beckoned to something deep and primal inside her, and she found herself lifting her hips to meet his next thrust. The movement brought him to her very core, and Dalton cried out, sharply, in a tone so ringing with pleasure that Angie shivered with delight. She understood at last the true miracle, the renewing circle of life, as man and woman came together in the age-old way to create life.

She felt a pang of regret that there would be no child from this union, and another at the thought of a tiny, dark-haired, green-eyed baby. But then Dalton slipped his hand between them and caressed her in a way that made her forget everything except the heat of his body and the touch of his hand. She lifted her hips again, straining, breathing harshly now, knowing that the final answer was within her reach, as long as Dalton didn't stop that slick, sliding caress, as long as he continued to fill her with the thick, hard flesh that was driving her to the brink of madness.

She felt him hesitate, frozen above her. Then a sharp, hissing gasp broke from him and he drove deep, gripping her shoulders to brace her for his forceful thrust. He cried out her name as his body arched, his head thrown back, his hips grinding hard against her.

He was the most beautiful thing she had ever seen—in all of her travels, in all of her years—and the sight of him, of the sheer, undiluted pleasure that drew his face taut, and the feel of him as he erupted into her, flooding her with liquid heat, sent her spiraling upward, her body gathering itself until his last convulsive movement shattered her. His name ripped from her throat as she clenched around him, tightly, drawing another cry from him, but she was barely aware of it over the waves of hot, rippling sensation that swept her.

He collapsed atop her, panting, his arms wrapped around her shoulders, his long legs tangled with hers, his slowly ebbing flesh still inside her.

And as Angie looked at him, marveled over the pure male beauty of him, and at what he had just shown her, she wondered how long it was going to take her to make up for what she'd missed.

A last echoing shudder rippled through Dalton. The sheer intimacy of what had happened overwhelmed him. He couldn't look at her. He kept his face buried in the curve of her neck and shoulder, knowing he couldn't meet her gaze, not after this. It was all he could do to speak.

"Why, Angie?"

He felt her go very still beneath him. "Why?"

"You know what I mean." He hadn't meant to sound harsh, but it came out that way anyway.

"I . . . didn't think it mattered."

His head came up then. He stared at her incredulously. "You didn't think it mattered that you were a virgin?"

Her eyes were calm as she looked up at him. "It was my decision, Dalton. And one I've waited a very long time to make. I'm not sorry. Don't you be."

He nearly groaned out loud. He didn't need this. He didn't *want* this. There was too much responsibility in being a woman's first man. That was why he'd never done it before, despite the energetic efforts of a few teenage groupies in the past. He'd said it was because they were jail bait, but in truth it had been more because he didn't find much that was attractive in women who found their self-esteem in whom they slept with—the hottest new race car driver, in his case.

So now what was he supposed to do?

Angie sighed and tightened her arms around him in a hug. "Thank you, Dalton. I finally understand."

"Understand?" he repeated warily.

"Mmm-hmm. I never did, before. I mean, I always did fine, up to a point. But because I never knew how powerful it could be, I could never seem to anticipate what people would do when love came into the picture."

Dalton stopped breathing for a long moment. "Angie," he said, his voice brittle. "This was not love. It was sex, pure and simple."

She blinked, as if puzzled. "Well, I know it was sex, but—"

"Don't try to make anything more out of it. I wanted it, so did you, so we scratched the itch. That's all."

He yanked himself away from her, overbalancing and winding up on the floor of the car, giving his bum ankle a wrench that made him wince. Damn it, he should have known she would have to dress it up and make it pretty. That was the trouble with virgins, once they gave it up, they had to convince themselves they'd only done it because they were in love. Well, *he* wasn't in love. He never would be. He understood that and accepted it. She would just have to accept it, too, because he wouldn't change it even if he could.

He shifted, trying to get up, but he was caught at an awkward angle on the floor between the seats, his legs too long to let him maneuver easily.

"Damn," he swore under his breath. "I'm too old for this."

"For what?"

Her voice was so calm that he looked up at her in surprise. He'd expected her to be hurt when he'd bluntly classified what had happened between them as merely sex. In his gut, he knew it was much more than that, but his mind veered away from the fact like a race car with a blown tire had once veered into him.

Her expression was as calm as her voice had sounded. And she was looking at him expectantly, waiting for an answer.

"What do you think?" he snapped. "We're in the back seat of a car, for God's sake, my jeans are around my ankles and your dress isn't even off. You'd think we were a couple of hormone-laden teenagers."

"Is that so bad?" she asked with an innocence he would have sworn was unfeigned. Then, incredibly, she smiled. A wide, teasing smile that flicked at something deep inside him, something that had been frozen for so long he'd forgotten it existed. "I'm sure I'm not the only one to have had her first time in the back of this car."

He stared at her in wonder. What was that she'd said, about not being able to anticipate what people would do? Well right now he was so bewildered by her reaction he didn't know what to say. The memory of another time when he also hadn't known what to say—incredibly, less than an hour ago—rose in his mind, only to be quashed immediately. He wasn't ready to deal with that yet. For that matter, he wasn't ready to deal with this, either. The only thing he was ready to do was get away.

"It's all right, Dalton," she said quietly. She reached over to lay a gentle hand on his arm. "You don't have to run from feeling alive."

He went rigid. It was as if she'd dug down into his shriveled soul with her gentle touch, and found the core of his agitation.

"Damn you," he rasped, "whatever you're doing, stop it."

"You have a right to be happy, you know."

The whip of guilt snapped, stinging a sharp retort out of him. "Like hell I do."

He scrambled out of the car, yanked his jeans up and zipped them.

"Get dressed," he ordered. "I'm going to open the door so you can get out of here."

Still her expression of calm never wavered. With a dignity he would have thought impossible under the circumstances, she gracefully climbed out of the car and fixed her clothing, the barely noticeable trembling in her fingers as she began to button the dress the only outward sign that anything was unusual.

He watched her, his jaw clenched. His body tightened fiercely at the sight of the curved flesh of her breasts disappearing behind the soft fabric. It was just that it had been so long, he told himself. He would have felt this way with any woman, after all this time without release.

She finished at last, and lifted her gaze to his face. God, how could she look at him like that? How could she look at him as if she'd heard none of the cutting, harsh things he'd said? Or as if she'd heard them, but they didn't matter. As if she understood the deepest, darkest reasons for his sudden coldness, reasons he wasn't sure he understood himself? He only knew that what had happened between them had been too intense, that things were tumbling far too fast, that he needed some time and space to regain his balance.

And to convince himself that this idea of some sort of inexplicable mental connection between them was totally crazy.

Nine

___

Angie rolled over in bed and, grudgingly, opened her eyes in surrender; she obviously wasn't going to get any more sleep tonight. She had initially dozed off quickly enough, so wonderfully satiated had her body been, but she'd awakened in the gray light of predawn. And had been awake ever since, aware only of her sadness at Dalton's resistance to letting go of that burden of guilt, to coming out of the lonely, isolated life he'd condemned himself to.

Then the not unpleasant soreness of certain intimate parts of her body reminded her that this haunted, withdrawn man had given her a miraculous gift of knowledge, a knowledge that even the bosses hadn't been able to give her. A knowledge she wondered if they, in their superior but sometimes detached wisdom, were even capable of understanding.

The bosses.

She sat up sharply. Her hand instinctively went to the pendant, but it was still dead, cool and silent to the touch. Just as well, she thought gratefully. If they'd decided to reconnect tonight, while she'd been—

Lord, even if they had, she wouldn't have noticed. She'd been incapable of noticing anything amid the storm of sensations that Dalton had caused in her. Color and heat flooded her cheeks, and she pressed her hands to her face in the darkness. Next time she would take the pendant off.

If, of course, there was a next time.

She fingered the gold charm, wondering if she had been deserted altogether. Were the bosses finally fed up with her? Had they written her off?

If they hadn't already, she thought wryly, they certainly had cause now. Of course, they didn't know that, yet.

But if they *had* truly abandoned her permanently, they wouldn't just leave her here, would they? They had always said it was a one-way deal, that if she quit, she'd wind up right back where they'd found her. It was a surefire way of guaranteeing loyalty.

Well, there was one way to find out. If they'd abandoned her, she'd be powerless now. She knew they would never leave her that, if they truly had deserted her.

She looked across the room at the stack of school papers she had yet to grade. Immediately she knew Jimmy's was halfway down the stack; she could see the bold if slightly crooked scrawl of his writing as if it were suspended in front of her. She shifted her gaze to the doll that sat on the bureau, one of the multitude of Mrs. Webster's collection that cluttered the house. She concentrated and, after a moment, the doll tilted, then toppled over, protected from damage by the stiff fullness of the lace petticoat.

So far, so good. Angie closed her eyes and probed close at hand. The response was immediate; Lilah Webster was sound asleep, not even dreaming at the moment.

Now for the acid test, she thought.

By the time she realized that if she were going to test this stronger power, she ought to be testing it on Jimmy, she had already reached out to Dalton. It was a much greater distance, to that painfully tidy little room over the garage, but when the connection clicked in, it was as clear as if he were in the same room with her. Once she got through the chaos of his still spinning thoughts, she got the sense of the same sleeplessness she'd been suffering, the same physical awareness of a body unused to lovemaking and a mind shocked at the sweetness of it....

And then it hit her, a swirling mass of heated memories, vivid images of his body sliding over hers, into hers, of her soft, wondering cries, and she realized with a little shock that she was feeling what he had felt as he had driven himself into her with an urgency that left her breathless—then, and now. It was incredible. She felt the heat boiling up inside her, felt the pulsing throb of need as the two bodies etched with vivid clarity in her mind approached that consuming climax.

Even as her body responded to the power of the feeling, she realized with no little amount of awe that in this glowing vision she was both taker and taken, and perhaps the only woman alive who truly knew what the man who had made love to her had experienced.

Damn it, Angie, stop it!

She gasped out loud. Immediately every shield, every safeguard snapped into place, severing the bond that should never have existed in the first place.

This was impossible. It had never, ever happened before. As far as she knew, it had never happened with any

of the bosses' operatives. Reading a person not directly
connected to a mission was difficult enough; having the
connection go both ways was unheard of.

She clasped the pendant, but it remained cool and still.
She tried sending a message, anyway, but the familiar hum
and slight vibration didn't materialize.

None of this made any sense. They'd seemingly deserted her, yet had left her her powers. What happened
now? Surely they wouldn't just leave her like this. One of
the main reasons for their success rate over all these years
of doing this was the fact that they remained unknown and
unremembered when the task at hand was finished. Only
that secrecy had allowed them to function so freely, and so
successfully.

They couldn't possibly just leave her here, not with all
the knowledge she held. Even if they *had* relented, decided to make an exception in her case and not put her
back where they'd found her, they would have erased her
memory of them, and of everything she'd done since
they'd saved her for their own purposes.

So did this mean they would pop up again, reestablish-
ing the connection when they saw fit? Would it be soon, or
would she be going about whatever her business might be,
years from now, and then the pendant would thrum to life,
recalling her?

She wrestled with the seemingly unanswerable question
all day as she struggled to get through her classes without
remembering that amazing mental joining, that moment
when Dalton's memories had become hers and she'd felt
his remembered responses as if they were her own.

And every time her guard was down and those images
crept in again, the connection was there. Dalton was there.
She no longer had to even try; all she had to do was unintentionally think about him, and his consciousness in-

vaded hers and she had to slam the doors of her mind. It
was up to her to do that, she sensed; Dalton had no idea
how to control this. She also sensed he was beginning to
wonder about his sanity.

He was getting scared.

And, she thought wearily as the last class of the day—
Jimmy's class—filed in, from her experience, when men
got scared, they got angry. And right now the last thing she
needed was an angry Dalton MacKay. For, she admitted
ruefully, her own sake as much as Jimmy's.

But no explanation she could give Dalton would suf-
fice. This was too strange, too impossible.

Of course, she thought as she tapped a pencil idly on her
desk, she could always just tell him the truth. Her mouth
quirked; that should go over well.

She was distracted throughout the class—as was Jimmy,
she noticed—but the other students were so primed and
enthusiastic about the history they'd once groaned about
that she barely had to do anything to keep the discussion
moving. She'd accomplished that, at least. And she'd en-
joyed it; perhaps, had she continued in her other life, she
would have become a teacher.

No, she thought wryly, she never would have made it,
not then. The opinions that she'd always held, opinions
that fit into the world view now, would have made her a
bluestocking at best then, and at worst, an outcast, a
woman who didn't know her place.

And just what, she thought glumly, is different now?
Aren't you exactly that, a woman who doesn't know where
she belongs?

"You okay, Jimmy?" she asked when the class was finally over and the students began to leave—still, she
thought proudly, arguing about whether the Tories should
have been allowed to go free after the war was over.

The boy shrugged. "Yeah."

She remembered then, and apologized silently to the boy for her forgetfulness. "Good luck at your meeting with the social worker tonight."

For an instant, fear sparked in his eyes. Then, with an effort that was visible—at least to her—he fought it down. "They're gonna do what they're gonna do," he said carelessly.

She'd thought she'd reassured him, but apparently he needed a bit more. "They're going to do what you make them do, Jimmy. You, by what you do, how you act, will determine what they decide."

His eyes widened. "I . . . never thought of it like that."

"Think about it, Jimmy."

"Yeah. Yeah, I will."

He turned to go, reached the door, then looked back over his shoulder at her, grinning.

"You got company, teacher."

Angie heard the deep tones of a man just outside the door as he, as she had, wished Jimmy good luck tonight. She stood there, frozen, unable to move, not needing to see, not even needing to expand her senses; she knew it was Dalton.

When he stepped through the classroom door, she almost forgot to breathe. He was as beautiful as she remembered, his long legs clad in a pair of snug black jeans that scrunched up over black boots. He wore a white, long-sleeved, button-down shirt, with the sleeves rolled up over muscled forearms. The loose fit of the shirt only emphasized the leanness of his hips and the flatness of his belly.

He also looked haggard, weary...and as she had feared, both scared and angry.

"I need to talk to you. Alone."

His voice matched his expression. "I . . ." She knew she couldn't deny him. "All right."

"Not here."

"All right," she repeated.

"My place."

For a man who needed to talk, he surely wasn't doing much of it now, she thought. But she merely said a third time, "All right." Then she added, "I have to turn in some paperwork—"

"I'll wait there."

She nodded, and without another word he turned on his booted heel and walked out of the room. This was not, she thought with a sigh, going to be pleasant.

When she arrived at the garage, to her surprise it was closed. She walked up the outside stairs to the door of the room above and knocked; nothing. She stood there for a moment, pondering, then heard footsteps on the concrete of the garage driveway. They were slightly uneven, and when she caught a glimpse of him, she realized he was limping.

He glanced up and saw her, and started up the stairs.

"I guess I drove faster than you." Her attempt at a quip fell flat.

"I walked. I don't have a car. I don't drive."

A car mechanic who didn't have a car? A former race car driver who didn't drive? True, she hadn't heard a car, or ever seen one here that he wasn't working on, but it seemed odd that when he wound up limping after less than a mile-long walk, he didn't own some kind of transportation. Especially if, as Maggie Kirkland had said, he made house calls.

She stepped back as he brushed past her and reached for the doorknob. She was startled when he simply turned it and the door swung open.

"You don't have a key, either?"

"Nothing worth stealing."

And you wouldn't care if it happened. She had, she thought grimly, overestimated how pleasant this was going to be.

She stepped inside when he gestured her ahead of him; at least he wasn't so angry he'd discarded his manners. The room looked much as she'd seen it that first night. Painfully clean and neat, and lacking in anything that might make it less anonymous. As if he'd kept it this way to remind himself he wasn't worth anything better, Angie thought.

The door shut with a slam. She barely managed not to jump. He walked past her—not limping now, she noticed, although the set of his jaw suggested he was controlling it at some cost—then turned to face her. He didn't comment on the room, or how he must know it appeared to strangers. He'd so thoroughly shut himself off from everything else, she supposed he didn't care about that, either.

"I want to know what the hell is happening. What you're doing to me, and how you're doing it."

So much for small talk, she thought. Playing ignorant was obviously out of the question; he knew as well as she did something was going on. Besides, she didn't think she could do that to him, despite doubting that the fact that she was just as confused about it as he was was going to help her much.

"I don't know what's happen—"

He swore sharply, pungently, cutting her off. "Don't lie."

She took in a deep breath. "Let me put that differently. I don't know *why* it's happening. I only know ... I'm not doing anything to make it happen."

And that was the honest truth, now. All she had to do was think about him for more than ten seconds—something she did all too often—while her guard was down, and the connection was there.

He let out a long breath, and she saw a flicker of relief flash in his eyes, lighting the shadowed green for an instant. He'd been afraid she would deny it was happening at all, she realized. And then he'd be faced with the possibility that he was truly losing his mind. She was grateful she hadn't tried to deny it.

She watched him pace the room. He came to a halt in front of the narrow bed against the wall. She followed him, wondering where all her easy words had vanished to. Apparently that was another thing she'd never understood; it was easy to know what to say when it wasn't your heart that was involved. And she could no longer deny that her heart was most definitely involved with this man.

"This morning," he said slowly, "just before dawn, I..."

"I know," she said when he trailed off, heat flooding her anew at the memory. "I mean it, Dalton. I don't know why this is happening. It's never happened to me before."

He turned then, facing her. "It's as if...you can slip into my mind." His sense of anger at the intimate violation swept over her, and she couldn't blame him one bit.

"And vice versa," she observed, a little defensive in the face of his repulsion.

That seemed to slow him down a little. "Today," he said, "I kept getting bits and pieces. I'd be working, and suddenly there you were. I'm not even sure how I knew it was you."

"I understand," she said honestly. "The same thing happened to me."

He studied her for a silent minute that became two, then three. Then, almost desolately, "You're really not doing it, are you?"

"Not intentionally. It...scares me. Not knowing what's going on."

He expelled a long, compressed breath. "Yeah, tell me about it."

"I thought maybe it was because...we made love," she said, using the gentler term almost defiantly. "But then I remembered the connection was there...before that."

He had drawn back a little at her first words, but then he nodded. "When I couldn't think of what to say to Jimmy, when he was talking about his dreams, I thought of you, wished you were here, to tell me what to say. And then...you did."

He grimaced, as if knowing how ridiculous that sounded. She wondered how he would feel if she told him the connection had started long before then.

"How did you know?" he asked. "How did you even know what we were talking about?" He bit his lip and turned his head away from her. "God, I'm talking like this was some logical thing. If you can climb into my mind, then of course you would know what we were talking about."

There was a look in his eyes that was a little wild. She wanted to probe, just for an instant, just for a clue as to what she should do, but she didn't trust her ability to keep it one-way anymore, to keep him from knowing what she was doing.

Reflexively, even though she expected no answer, she fingered the pendant. It was still dead. It would be too much to ask, she thought wryly, that they pop up at a time that would be convenient for her.

"You always seem to be wearing that charm," he said suddenly, like a man grasping at any question that might have a reasonable answer. "Why a steamboat?"

She hadn't expected that question, but was grateful for the change of subject. Until she realized it could open up a line of questioning no easier to answer. She opted for the literal answer about the golden charm.

"It's a side-wheeler. Like the ones that ran the Mississippi in the old days."

"You're always touching it. Does it mean something special to you?"

That, she could never explain. She borrowed a tactic she had seen so many women use over the years, for the first time understanding why they did it: she tried to deflect the unwanted questions with an attack.

"Does it matter? I got the impression you didn't want me to think you cared enough to ask about that kind of thing."

He flushed slightly. "I didn't mean that. I just didn't want you to think..."

His voice trailed off awkwardly.

"That you loved me? I didn't, Dalton. If you'd given me a chance, I would have told you that I didn't expect anything from you."

He winced, as if her words hurt him in a way he'd never expected. "Why, Angie? You're what, twenty-six or seven? Why did you wait all that time and then..."

"Give myself to you in the backseat of a car?"

The flush returned to his cheeks, darkening them to a dull red. "Yes," he said, his voice tight.

"Because," she said simply, knowing he had no idea just how special this made him, "you're the only man I've ever met that made me want to." She held his gaze levelly. "You still are."

He sucked in an audible breath.

"It's all right," she said quietly. "I understand. I truly don't expect anything from you."

"And that's the biggest why of all," he muttered. "You deserve better than..."

"Than you?" He nodded, not meeting her eyes. "Perhaps." Her tone was mild. "But it doesn't matter, since I don't want anyone else."

His head came up sharply then. "Are you saying you still— What *are* you saying?"

"I'm saying it's up to you, Dalton. I've told you I understand. That I don't expect you to...love me." It hurt just to say it. Even knowing it was impossible for so many reasons, she wished, just for this moment, that things were different. That Dalton wasn't so closed up and cold inside, that she could stay long enough to break him out of that flinty shell of isolation.

But perhaps she could. She'd been deserted, hadn't she? Perhaps they simply meant to leave her here. Perhaps she would have all the time in the world to try to free Dalton MacKay and bring him back to life.

The thought of day after day with him, loving him, convincing him he was worthy of being loved, made her heart seem to expand in her chest. But on the heels of that thought came thoughts of night after night with him. Here, even, on that narrow bed behind him. There was so much more she wanted to know, she wanted to learn how to make him feel as he'd made her feel, she wanted to know if his nipples were as sensitive as hers, if caressing them would make him feel as she did. She wanted to look at him, at that beautiful body, wanted to see him naked and aroused, and then she wanted to touch him, to learn what he liked, what would make him writhe beneath her hands...and then her mouth. Echoes of the sensations he'd aroused in her made her pulse race and her body begin to heat.

The connection leapt between them, and she knew her erotic speculations had cost her; she'd let her guard down—and let him in. Before she could consciously slam the doors in her mind, Dalton was in front of her, his hands coming up to grip her shoulders.

"God, Angie, do you have any idea what that does to me? To know what you're thinking, to know that you're getting hot at just the thought of touching me, to know what you want to do to me?" He gave a sound that was half harsh laugh, half groan. "It makes me forget every vow I've ever made, every reason I've ever had for staying alone. Hell, it makes me want to strip and lie down for you, so you can do everything you were just thinking of."

I wish you would, she thought, then gasped as she realized he was still reading her. His fingers tightened on her shoulders. And then he released her, backing up a step. Her breath leapt to her throat and was choked off as, his eyes fastened on hers, he began to unbutton his shirt.

Ten

Dalton tried to remind himself that this had been his idea. He had, after all, done willingly what she'd wished of him. He'd stripped and offered his body up to her for all the exploration she'd craved, so he had no right to whimper about it now.

But whimpering was what he was doing; she was killing him. He'd never guessed how her tentative touches would inflame him, or how the change from tentative to confident and daring would turn that flame into a conflagration. He was beyond caring that his entire body was trembling, beyond worrying about the groans that broke from him every time she discovered a new place that made him jump, beyond thinking of anything except hanging on to the edges of his narrow bed with both hands, whether to keep himself from grabbing her or to keep from bucking so wildly beneath her that he'd throw them both to the floor, he didn't know.

Nothing like this had ever happened to him, even in his wildest days on the race circuit. Because, he thought with the tiny part of his mind that was still functional, no one like Angie had ever happened to him. And no amount of telling himself he didn't deserve either one, the pleasure or the woman giving it to him, could slow down the avalanche of sensation she'd unleashed.

And when at last he broke, when at last he could take no more, when he knew he was going to explode with the next touch, her name became a litany on his lips as he pulled her beneath him and claimed the haven he'd never thought to find in this life.

She cried out when he slid home with one fierce thrust, but it wasn't pain, it was a cry of his name that was so sweet he nearly lost control right then. Only his need to be sure she was with him enabled him to hold back, and he shifted his hips to be certain his swollen flesh stroked the core of her with every movement. He felt her tremble. Or it could have been him; he wasn't sure. Nor did it matter; nothing mattered except the feel of her, accepting him, welcoming him. Welcome. It had been so long since he'd felt welcome. He drove deep, half afraid the feeling would vanish. It only heightened when she accepted his invasion with a joyous cry of his name.

The moment she lifted her legs and wrapped them convulsively around his waist, lifting her hips to drive him to the very heart of her, he knew he was lost. He felt the explosion boiling up inside him, and in the instant he surrendered to it he heard her cry out. Her deep, inner muscles contracted fiercely at the precise moment his flesh was expanding to its fullest. He nearly screamed at the intensity of it, and clutched at her desperately as wave after wave racked him.

And when he collapsed atop her, gasping, Dalton MacKay knew he would never be the same. He tried not to question the gift, but he couldn't help wondering what the price would be for this joy he didn't deserve.

You have a right to be happy, you know.

Angie's words rang in his ears, and for the first time since Mick's death, he wavered. In his sated, exhausted state, he had the oddest thought: Angie wouldn't be here with him if she didn't care, and she wouldn't care if he wasn't worth it. Not Angie. She was too wise, too caring herself to waste her time and her spirit.

But before he could dwell on that surprising idea, she was moving again, and proving to him that he wasn't nearly as exhausted as he'd thought.

For the first time Angie felt she was truly learning what it meant to be a woman. Being a woman meant loving the differences between male and female, and how perfectly they complemented each other. Being a woman meant thrilling to the sight of a special male body, beautiful in its strength. And being even more thrilled at the knowledge that she had the power to arouse that body.

And it meant appreciating his restraint, his holding back and letting her do as she wished to him, because it was what she wanted, when he'd been aching to take over and sate the urgent need she was creating in both of them.

Being a woman meant loving the taut look of need on one man's face. Savoring the low, husky sounds of pleasure he made when she stroked the right place in the right way. And taking the cry that broke from him when he erupted into the depths of her body, a cry that seemed to her like the sound of a barrier breaking, and knowing she would hold it in her heart forever.

And once again, it was Dalton who had taught her, Dalton who was still showing her what she'd never understood.

She crouched over him on the narrow bed, running her hand yet again over the ridged flatness of his sweat-sheened belly, then down until her fingers tangled in the thicket of hair surrounding the part of him that was so eager, so ready for her. She felt the deep muscles ripple, then felt his hips move convulsively beneath her thighs.

She'd been too shy to speak before, but this time she asked, "You . . . like that?"

"I think you discovered that—" his breath caught as she pressed slightly harder "—the last time."

She smiled at him. "Yes, but I missed a few places. A few very important places," she said, sliding her hand along the outside of his muscular thigh, then tracing a path back up the inside. She saw his belly tighten again in the instant before she heard his rapid intake of breath. Then, as she reached her goal and cupped rounded male flesh gently in her hands, he let out that breath in a fervent hiss of pleasure.

"Yes-s-s."

Angie smiled again. "Yes, I missed this before, or yes, it's important?"

"Both," he groaned, his eyes closing as his head pressed back into the pillow beneath him, making the cords of his neck stand out with the urgent strain.

She massaged and caressed him tentatively, until he pressed upward against her hand in a silent plea. Then she shifted, her hand moving upward, her fingers curling around him as she hadn't dared to before. He arched upward like a drawn bow, a hoarse cry breaking from his throat as she squeezed and stroked.

"You're so smooth," she said in awe. "And hot. And hard."

As if to test her own words, she slid her hand up and down his length, then again, quicker this time, touching him as if she'd never felt anything so wondrous.

"It doesn't seem possible," she murmured, circling him again with eager fingers, "that you fit inside me."

"Angie," he began warningly.

She stopped, and he reached for her. She twisted out of his grasp.

"Uh-uh," she said, shaking her head. "Now I get to start over."

"Over?" he said a little weakly. "I thought you just did."

"That was just touching. Now I have to learn kissing. In all the same places."

His eyes widened, and she didn't need to probe to see that he was remembering all those places. And imagining her mouth on them. He groaned, low and deep and husky with anticipation.

"I'm not going to last through this," he predicted grimly.

She began slowly, blazing paths with her lips and following them with her tongue. In minutes he was twisting beneath her mouth, breath coming in audible gulps. She explored every inch of him, tasting now everything she had touched before.

In fact, he lasted until she caressed the tip of his distended male flesh with her lips. Then he came up off the narrow bed in a rush, grabbing her at the waist. She shivered with heated sensation when she felt his fingers probing at her body, and shivered again with emotion when she realized that even now, as he growled that she'd driven him completely out of his mind, he was making sure she was ready, so he wouldn't hurt her.

"It's a damn good thing," he muttered as he found her slick and wet, "because I can't wait another second."

He proved his words then, lifting her swiftly over him.

"Help me," he rasped, sweat beading up once more on his forehead.

She reached down to grasp him, guiding him to her. The instant the tip of him began to arrow home, he brought her down hard on him, making her gasp at the sudden, thrilling shock of it. He cried out her name as she sheathed him, arching his hips up off the bed to drive himself fiercely home.

She felt as if she'd captured some wild, uncontrollable beast who nevertheless was taking her where she wanted to go. She held on, barely hearing her own moans, her attention fastened on the hot green of his eyes, the sleek, satin-over-muscle feel of his skin, the guttural cries that tore from him at the depth of each stroke, and the incredible, hot thickness of him pounding into her.

She savored the knowledge that, at least in these moments, Dalton was thoroughly, completely alive. Alive and teaching her yet another truth; as good as it had been, it could get even better.

Angie awoke slowly, reluctantly relinquishing the feeling of soft, warm contentment. The room was still warm with the heat of the afternoon sun, but the light was changing, on the edge of fading as twilight approached.

Twilight.

She was widely, rigidly awake now. It wasn't morning, and she wasn't in her own room. She was naked, and curled up with Dalton MacKay on his narrow bed. Other memories rushed back, and the comfortable warmth she'd been feeling rapidly became heat.

She shifted slightly to look at him. He didn't seem to find it odd to sleep in the afternoon. He'd seemed to welcome it. Not, she thought ruefully, that they'd had any choice. He'd made his earlier words come true, and they had made love until they were too exhausted to move. He had, as promised, fallen asleep still buried inside her—and it had been the most miraculous feeling of her life.

She reached out to gently smooth back the stubborn lock of dark hair that always wanted to flop over his forehead, near the scar, then stopped; she didn't want to wake him. He so rarely slept at all, she couldn't bear to disturb this peaceful slumber.

She lay back down, snuggled up to him, her cheek pressed against his chest, and tried to return to that marvelously sleepy state.

She became aware of the acceleration of his pulse first through the pounding of his heart under her cheek. She thought at first he was awake—she'd certainly felt his heart take off like this before, when she'd been indulging her desire to learn every spot on his body that made him gasp when she caressed it—but realized quickly that he still slept.

His breathing also quickened, and she realized he was dreaming. She wondered about what, and thought for an instant about probing to find out. She discarded the idea immediately; she couldn't possibly invade him like that, not when she knew how it disturbed him. Not after this afternoon.

Besides, it didn't seem to be a bad dream. In fact, he seemed almost to be smiling. He was—

His eyes came open, sleepily, as hers had. And then, instantly, he sat up rigidly beside her. A low sound, a gut-deep moan of despair, broke from him. She felt the emotion that drove it, knew it was ripping away at him with heedless, bloody claws.

She couldn't bear it. She reached out to take his hands.

"A bad dream?" she asked softly, sending every bit of calm and warmth and safety she had to him.

Slowly, a bit dazedly, he stared down at her fingers, clasped around his. His lashes lifted, and his eyes met hers. She thought he was going to resist, thought he might just be the one strong enough to do it...and then he broke and let her in.

"No," he said at last, the words coming in short bursts. "The dream isn't bad. It's ... good. In the dream ... everything goes right. I'm down on the line. I see the hole. I punch it. And then I'm through, in the lead ... and Mick is right behind me ...I can tell he's grinning at me ... then..."

She read the rest, without words, without any special power. Then he woke up and the truth flooded back. Bringing with it a morass of guilt he'd been carrying for years now. His dream was heaven; his hell was reality.

"You didn't kill him, Dalton. It was an accident."

He shook his head, denying the amelioration.

"You couldn't control the fact that someone else's tire blew out."

He didn't question her knowledge; he was too deep in his own pain. She eased up on the energy she was sending him; he was talking on his own now, and after keeping it bottled up for so long, she didn't think he'd be able to stop.

"I shouldn't have tried it. There was no margin for error. Or accident."

"Dalton—"

He turned on her then. "Don't you get it? I believed what they said. 'The hottest driver to come along in decades.' 'He doesn't take chances, he makes them.' 'He'll dominate racing for the next decade.' I ate it up. I ate it up, and when I saw that hole, my ego took me right through it. I was Dalton MacKay, the greatest thing since the internal combustion engine, of course I could do it."

He stopped, his eyes closing as his breath came in labored pants.

"I did it all right." His voice was laced with self-condemnation. "I sent Mick right into that wall."

"Dalton, please, listen to me—"

He wasn't hearing her. The demons were loose, lashing at him. The walls were well and truly down now, and the flood couldn't be stopped.

"He was the only person who ever really believed in me, who ever looked at me and saw something good, not just a troublemaker, not just some kid who never even knew who his parents were. I never cared much about anything, until Mick came along and taught me about racing. He was the closest thing to a father I ever had. And I killed him."

Angie hesitated, searching for the right thing to do, to say. "So the other drivers said you were responsible for his death," she said at last.

Dalton grimaced, opening his eyes to look at her. "No. They didn't. They all said it was a fluke, just a racing accident."

"Linda, then? She blamed you?"

Something flashed in his eyes then, puzzlement at her knowledge, but the dam had been breached now, and the words kept coming.

"No. That was the worst. She just kept telling me it wasn't my fault. And that . . . I was the son she and Mick had never had. She'd lived thirty years around racing, she said. She knew accidents like that happened."

"But she abandoned you. Didn't want anything to do with you."

"No!" His fists tightened until his knuckles were white. "She didn't. She wouldn't. She kept coming around, trying to talk to me. And his brother...even Mick's father tried."

"But Dalton MacKay had set himself up as his own judge and jury," she said softly.

"Because I *knew*," he said harshly. "I knew I only tried that move because I was an arrogant, conceited bastard who believed all his own publicity. And my ego cost Mick his life."

"And the only fair recompense was your own life. Of course, you couldn't just commit suicide, that would be too easy. So you sentenced yourself to a living hell, alone, every day of your life an installment on a debt you can never repay."

His jaw clenched, and he lowered his gaze to his fists, staring at them.

"Do you really think they want that, Dalton? That Mick's family appreciates what you're doing to yourself?"

His fists tightened until Angie thought he must be drawing blood from his palms. When she spoke again, she couldn't keep everything she'd come to feel for this man out of her voice. It was low and strained.

"Did you ever stop to think, Dalton, that if what Linda told you was true, then she lost not only a husband, but a son that day?"

His face went nearly as white as his knuckles. His breathing became louder, as if he was having to work for every breath. Anguish radiated from him, and Angie sensed the battle raging inside him. The dark and the light, the one he had consigned himself to, the other he thought he didn't deserve.

And suddenly it was too much for her. She couldn't bear to see him like this, was terrified the dark would win. She wrapped her arms around him and pulled him down to her, concentrating as she had never concentrated in her life on easing his pain. Nothing else mattered right now, except that she couldn't let this go on, couldn't let him keep ripping at himself, cursing himself, loathing himself.

He resisted at first, and she had to exert herself to build the shell of calm, of peace, around him. But she held on, murmuring soothing words she knew he wasn't listening to, but that wasn't important, only the sound was, only the sound and the tranquilizing softness, the gentle, warming, flowing current of serenity from her to him, reassuring, easing, cosseting, born of the love for him that she had only admitted to in this moment.

Minutes passed as she fought for him, using every ounce of power she had, every method she'd ever been taught. She knew she had broken through when he sagged against her, clutching at her as if she were his only support, his only lifeline in a raging sea.

"I loved him," he choked out brokenly. "Damn it, Angie, I loved him."

"I know," she whispered. She thought of the picture she'd seen and the look on Mick Graham's face. The knowledge came to her suddenly, almost as if the bosses were back. She tightened her hold on Dalton's shoulders. "And he knew, too, Dalton. He knew you loved him."

"I . . . never told him."

"It doesn't matter. He knew. I swear to you he knew."

He clung to her for several long, silent moments. She felt the turmoil in him gradually subside. And at last, with a final shiver as the riotous emotions retreated, he lifted himself up to look at her.

"Who are you?" he asked, his voice taut.

"I'm Angie," she said simply.

"What you did, just now..."

"Dalton, don't."

"Don't what? Don't ask how you did it? Don't ask how you've done any of this? Don't ask how you managed to dig your way past every barrier I could build? Don't ask—"

"Don't ask questions I can't answer."

He drew back from her a little on the narrow bed. His gaze flicked over their naked bodies, still pressed close together.

"I'm sorry, Dalton. I really am. I know it's awful of me, after...everything," she said, "but I can't. I just can't."

He looked back at her face then, but only for a moment. His gaze slipped down her throat, then lower, then stopped. His brows furrowed as he stared at something. At first she thought it was her breasts, and felt her nipples begin to tighten involuntarily. But then she realized he was looking higher.

And only then did she realize that, for the first time in days, the pendant was active. Not only active, but glowing, signaling her.

Great timing, she muttered silently. Absolutely great.

The pendant thrummed gently. Dalton's eyes widened, and she hastily grabbed at it and sent, rather violently, *Not now!*

Surprisingly they listened, and the thrumming subsided. She swiftly released it, and dared a glance at Dalton's face. And knew instantly that the lying, the evasion, was all over.

Already he had begun to withdraw from her, mentally and emotionally if not physically. It wouldn't take him long to have those walls back up, higher and thicker this time, and she doubted if anyone would ever get in again.

"Questions you can't answer," he muttered, his jaw tight.

He reached out and touched the pendant, surprise flickering over his face the moment his skin came in contact with it.

"It's warm," he murmured. "No, not just warm, it's...it's metal, but it feels..."

"I know," she said.

The surprise vanished from his expression, the coolness returning. He flicked at the pendant with a finger. It swung on its chain and came to rest backward against her skin. His eyes narrowed, and he leaned forward slightly.

"'*Sultana*. April 27, 1865,'" he read off the polished back of the pendant. His gaze came back to her face, and he waited silently. Tensely. As if the rest of his life depended on what she did next. And she knew, perhaps better than he, that it was true.

She couldn't let it happen. It didn't matter that she'd be wiped from his memory later, since it appeared the bosses were back. The only thing that mattered was this moment and the fact that the man she loved—Lord, the bosses weren't going to like this—had poured his battered soul out to her, at a cost she couldn't imagine, and she couldn't, wouldn't, let him wall himself back up again. Even if they erased his memory of her, those walls would be there if she didn't do something about it. Now.

She answered the easiest question first. "That's the day she exploded. On a run between St. Louis and New Orleans."

If he was relieved that she had answered at all, it didn't show. "An odd thing to want to commemorate."

"And odder still to wear it all the time?"

He nodded, with no lessening of that tension.

She took a breath, knowing how this was going to sound to him. But she had no choice.

"I wear it," she said, "because my family was wiped out in that explosion."

His brows furrowed. "I'm sorry. But not all of them, obviously. Somebody survived, because you're here."

Her nerve failed her for a moment. Perhaps she was starting this at the wrong end.

"Dalton, will you listen to a story?"

He was still more than a little wary, and she couldn't help thinking of that wounded wolf again, at the mouth of his den and scenting the air, wavering between taking the risk of stepping out into the sun, or retreating back into his dark, safe cave.

"What kind of a story?"

"The once-upon-a-time kind, I guess."

He looked doubtful, but he didn't say no, and she took a quick breath and plunged ahead before he could.

"A long, long time ago, a group of beings from a different place came across a world peopled by a developing race of creatures that they found very interesting. They stayed, initially simply to study these creatures, but they grew more and more fascinated as time went by. I think they were lonely, in a way. They saw great potential in these creatures, despite their primitiveness, and hoped that someday they would change, grow into something wonderful, perhaps even something similar to themselves. But then something would occur, some war or injustice, that made them think it would never happen."

He was listening, but she sensed his doubt was growing.

"I know this sounds crazy—"

"It sounds," he said flatly, "like you've been reading a bit too much science fiction."

"I know, but wait. Please."

"Get on with it, then," he said impatiently.

"These beings...they had laws that forbade them from interfering themselves. So instead they began to recruit people, the people of the race they'd been studying for so long."

"Is there a point to this fairy tale? And what does it have to do with that—" he gestured at the steamboat pendant "—and you?"

She sighed. "That day, when the *Sultana* blew up, there was a girl on board. She was seventeen, and traveling with her family."

Her voice tightened in spite of herself; Lord, was the old pain going to come back, too? She steadied herself and went on.

"Her parents, and her two brothers. They were all on a lower deck, talking about the man who'd murdered President Lincoln being caught the day before. That's when the explosion happened. They were all killed, before her eyes. The girl was badly hurt. She was dying, trapped on that lower deck as the boat went down."

"But she survived."

"Sort of."

"What does that mean?"

"I'm trying, Dalton. But this is hard. I've never told anyone this before. I'm breaking one of the primary rules by telling you."

He lapsed into silence then, waiting. After a moment she was able to go on.

"This girl, she had...a vision. At least, that's what she thought. She was in horrible pain, and the water was rising, and she knew she was about to die. And then a man appeared. He was dressed like a riverboat gambler, but he had the kindest eyes... He hadn't been a passenger on the boat, and he wasn't injured or even wet, but there he was. And he offered that girl a way out. A job, if she would agree to the conditions.''

As if unwillingly, Dalton made the logical guess. "You're saying he was one of those... recruiters?"

"Yes. They wanted the girl to do the interfering they couldn't do, according to their laws. To go where there was injustice, and make it right. To help those who'd never had their rightful chance. They would heal her, he said, and let her grow up a little first. And then they would give her the knowledge she needed. And the power to make things happen the right way.''

"Angie—''

"I know, it sounds wild, but please, let me finish. The girl agreed, she was hurting so much. She thought she was seeing things anyway, and her family was dead, so what did it matter if it was real or not? But the next thing she knew she was free of the wreckage. On the riverbank, looking back at it. And the pain was gone.''

Dalton was silent, but she sensed he was, albeit unwillingly, being drawn into the story. That gave her hope; the Dalton she'd first met would have thrown her out by now.

"She spent almost two months with them, learning the rules, and how to use the power they'd given her. Except that their time is different. That time equaled almost four years, back here.''

"The rest of this story is so ridiculous I won't even argue about that. What rules? What power?''

"They gave her vision. Enhanced perception, I suppose. The power of will, and the capability of extending it to others, to plant ideas, or make things happen. The ability to understand people, who they are, why they do what they do, even those who are . . . very practiced at hiding themselves. And some other things I can't quite explain."

Dalton went very still. "You mean, like reading thoughts? Like talking to someone when you're not even here?"

"Yes."

His voice went suddenly as harsh as it had been before she'd ever begun her story.

"You mean, like invading minds?"

"No!" She sat up as she told him urgently, "I don't know what's gone wrong, Dalton. It's never happened to me before, never in all the years I've been doing this. The connection isn't supposed to be like that, two-way, and it shouldn't be involuntary, but it is, all I have to do is think about you, and God knows I do that often enough, and there it is. I don't—"

"You're saying," he interrupted her in a deadly quiet voice, "that you're . . . What the hell *are* you saying? That you're some reincarnation of that girl?"

"No." She once more steadied herself, and then, making herself hold his gaze, she said simply, "I *am* that girl."

Dalton swore, low and heartfelt. She ignored it.

"I've been working for them ever since. The bosses sent me here to help Jimmy. That was all I was supposed to do. But you kept intruding. They told me to stay away from you, but I couldn't get you out of my mind."

"Do you have any idea," Dalton said slowly, "how totally insane this story sounds?"

"Yes."

He stared at her. Then he shook his head. "If it wasn't for the crazy way I've been feeling, and the way that necklace of yours started to glow . . . What is it, anyway?"

"It's my connection with the bosses. How I communicate with them."

"Right," he said sourly. "Wouldn't a wrist radio be easier?"

"Maybe I'll suggest it. But I want a fax, too," she quipped feebly. "That way I won't have to remember all their long-winded reports."

"Reports?"

"Background on a mission. A briefing, I guess you'd call it."

His eyes widened. "Is that how you knew about Linda?" Before she could go on, he was pelting her with questions. "What else do you know? And how the hell did you find out? What are you, really, a reporter or something? Looking to dig up an old tragedy for a new story?"

It was clear he wasn't convinced. She was going to have to give him more.

"No, Dalton," she said softly. "I'm exactly what I told you I am. And I know more than any reporter could ever find out. I know about the trash can in the hospital bathroom. I know that you were named for the hospital and the street it was on. I know that you were adopted once, but the man lost his job and they had to send you back. I know that you once lived with a big, blond man who beat you until you were bruised all over. I know that you torture yourself over and over with a videotape of Mick's crash—"

He jerked away from her then, rolling off the bed to come shakily to his feet. His injured ankle made him stagger, but he backed away from her hastily nevertheless.

"Nobody knows all that. *Nobody.*"

"I know. I picked it up from you, that day at the café." She sighed. "I honestly don't know what's gone wrong with me. Part of the procedure was to suppress my normal emotions. This work would be too hard, impossible in fact, if you felt things in the normal way. To learn to care, then have to leave, to go on endlessly, while those you've helped gradually die natural deaths.''

He just stood there, staring at her, and Angie had to repress the need to go to him, to hold him, to touch him, to stroke that beautiful male body once again. She forced herself back to her explanation. The explanation he wasn't believing.

"Since I've been working for them I've never felt sorrow, or stress, or emotional pain. But the night I came to Three Oaks, I started feeling them all." She met his stare levelly. "Starting with your anguish when you tried to write to Linda. That was the night I arrived."

She saw his belly muscles contract as if she'd struck him.

"I wasn't supposed to feel anything, Dalton. And then I met you, and all the rules went out the window."

"You expect me to believe this?"

"How else could I know all those things?"

He shook his head sharply, as if trying to clear it. "What rules?"

She blinked. "What?"

"You mentioned rules. And that you were breaking a big one by telling me this . . . tall tale."

Dutifully, even knowing he wouldn't believe her, she recited them. "No violence. No lying, except by omission or when necessary to keep to the rest of the rules. No interference with anything that doesn't have a direct bearing on your mission." She gave him a wry smile. "I've been having a little trouble with that one lately."

His expression changed slightly, as if he knew she'd meant because of him. But he only asked, "And the one you broke?"

She sighed. "That no one ever finds out who—or what—you are."

"Like anyone would believe it anyway," he muttered.

She'd done all she could do. Angie got to her feet and gathered up her clothes, pulling them on hastily, aware of his eyes on her and the fact that he was standing there, naked, giving her a full view of the body she'd loved from head to toe just a few hours ago.

"That's it?" he asked as he watched her make ready to go. "You just walk away, after that . . . story?"

"I've told you everything there is to tell. What you do about it is up to you." She picked up her purse. "But think about it, Dalton. Think about it and you'll see that there really is no other explanation for how I know what I know. And think about the fact that if I was going to lie, why on earth would I make up such a ludicrous one?"

She got to the door and started to open it. Then she turned back. "I was wrong. There is one more thing worth telling you. It wasn't supposed to happen, either. But it did. You can think about this, too."

"What?" he asked tiredly.

"I love you."

His eyes widened, and his face paled. Slowly, like a dazed animal, he shook his head, his stunned gaze never leaving her face. Her mouth twisted painfully.

"I didn't think you'd want it," she said tightly.

She pulled the door quietly shut behind her. She thought she heard her name, faint and anguished, and she waited, but the door stayed closed. She left, feeling more exhausted than she ever had in her life.

Eleven

When she got home she found that Jimmy had come looking for her four hours ago. Guilt swept her; she hadn't been there for him. He'd seemed upset, Mrs. Webster said. And more upset when he found out she was gone. He'd left on that bike of his, the older woman said, riding like a crazy person.

She dragged herself upstairs and collapsed into the big chair, castigating herself mercilessly. She'd selfishly been with Dalton, while the boy she was here to help had needed her. Remembering that that was about the time the bosses had signaled her, she felt even worse. She'd really done it now, she thought. The next time they called her, it would no doubt be to fire her.

Well, maybe she'd just save them the trouble.

She reached for the pendant. The connection was so immediate she knew they'd been waiting. Fine, now that she'd made an irretrievable jumble out of things.

Where have you been? What have you been doing all this time?

Ah, we've been . . . busy.

Odd, she thought. If they were human, she would have thought they were equivocating.

Evangeline—

Don't bother telling me. I know I've messed up everything.

Well, things are a bit confused . . .

No. I really have messed up, this time. I guess I'm just not cut out for this work.

She meant it. She'd finally come to believe what they'd always told her. She was too headstrong to do this job well. She'd indulged herself, convinced herself that she could help both Jimmy and Dalton, and had instead wound up hurting them both.

Dear girl—

I should have let you pull me when you wanted to. Now you have to.

We do?

I told you. I've ruined everything. But please, don't give up on Jimmy because of me. He could be such a good kid, if you give him half a chance. Or send in someone who's good at this.

Evangeline, stop—

Look, I know that you were giving me one last chance to sink or swim. To prove myself. That's why you left me alone all this time, isn't it? Well, all I've proved is that I'm incompetent. You have to pull me and put in someone who can really help.

You're being much too hard on yourself.

She went on as if they hadn't answered.

Would you please do me one last favor? Would you . . . erase me from Jimmy's mind? And . . . Dalton's? I know I don't have any right to ask, but please? For their sake? Jimmy's already come to trust me a little, it would only make things worse for him if I just disappear. And Dalton—

She broke off, trying desperately to hide her pain.

He doesn't deserve this, she told them. Not more pain. He was starting to reach out, and then I—

Evangeline.

Her stomach knotted; it was the big boss.

Yes, sir.

It is too late to pull you now. And there is no one else available. You're going to have to finish this. And soon. It's up to you to save that boy. Do you understand?

But I—

It's time you stopped thinking about yourself, was the stern answer. *Think about that boy. The rest of his life hangs in the balance.*

She sat there clutching the pendant for a long time after the connection had been broken.

The tapping on her door was faint but definite.

"Evangeline?"

Angie sat up in her lonely, cold bed and yawned. She'd been a fool to even try going to sleep. You didn't sleep when you'd made a ruin out of two people's lives and your own.

The tapping came again. She shook her head. "Yes, Mrs. Webster. What is it?"

Through the closed door the elderly woman's voice was muffled. "Sorry to…Kirkland…Wants…talk… She's down…parlor."

Jimmy.

It had to be. Why else would Mrs. Kirkland be here at this hour?

She slid quickly out of bed and threw on a robe. She opened the door, apologized to Mrs. Webster about the intrusion and the late hour, then scurried downstairs.

Maggie Kirkland was sitting in a big, upholstered chair whose back and arms were covered with Mrs. Webster's ubiquitous crocheted doilies. She looked exhausted, not only in face and posture, but emotionally. Angie could feel the weariness coming off the woman in waves.

She crossed the room and knelt beside the chair.

"What is it, Maggie?" she asked softly. "Jimmy?"

Maggie looked up then, her eyes both tired and sad. "He's gone. I've been driving all over, looking for him. I tried the movie theater, the convenience store that has the video games...."

She shook her head wearily. "I even called the garage, but Mr. MacKay said he wasn't there. Bob had to stay in Santa Barbara tonight, and I didn't know who else to turn to. Jimmy seemed to like you so much, I thought he might have come to you."

Guilt stabbed at Angie anew. "He did. I...wasn't here."

Maggie Kirkland sighed. "I'm sure he's with those awful boys."

"What makes you think that?"

"He always goes out with them when he's angry."

"Mrs. Webster said he seemed upset. Did something go wrong at the meeting?"

"Not in the beginning. I was so proud of Jimmy, he was so calm, and well-behaved. He seemed like he'd done some real growing up. We were afraid when he saw Jimmy's grades, Mr. Power—that's the social worker—would take him away, so we took the work he's done in your class with us, to show he was trying more now. We tried to tell Mr. Power that, but he kept harping about everything that was going wrong instead of what was going right. Jimmy finally lost hope.''

Angie's heart sank. ''What did he do?''

''He tried to explain, but then he started looking sullen again, you know how he does. Then Mr. Power lectured him about his attendance at school, and told him that if he didn't shape up, he would land in juvenile hall. We would probably never see him again, then.''

''There are some who would say you'd be better off,'' Angie said gently.

''I know. Sometimes, God forgive me, I've even thought that myself. But it seems—so unfair, to give up on him now. I'd hoped he was turning around. He seemed so much happier, since Mr. MacKay came, and then when you came he even started to take an interest in school....''

Angie saw tears begin to well up in the woman's eyes. She reached out and laid her fingers atop the other woman's tightly knotted hands. She got a rush of the woman's exhaustion, and her genuine concern for the boy who had caused her so much grief. If Jimmy could just get past his anger, he could have a home here. A real home. This woman had more than enough love to give, and she had enough of a giver's heart to want to give it to this troubled boy.

''It's going to be all right, Maggie,'' Angie said softly. ''Go home. Get some rest. I'll find Jimmy.''

''But—''

''Don't you worry.'' She sent the woman a wave of reassurance, the strongest she could muster. ''Just get some rest. He'll be home by morning. I promise you.''

Looking somewhat puzzled, Maggie nodded, then stood. Angie led her to the door, then stood watching until she was safely inside the house across the street. Then she turned and raced back upstairs to pull on jeans, heavy socks under her athletic shoes, and a thick, warm, red sweater.

"That boy," Mrs. Webster, who was waiting by the front door when she came down, intoned severely, "is more trouble than he's worth."

Angie paused, looking at the older woman. "Sometimes I think the more they're worth, the more trouble they are, Mrs. Webster."

She only hoped Jimmy wouldn't make a liar out of her.

The Chevy coughed gently, and Angie glanced at the dash. "I don't have time for this," she muttered, glaring at the needle of the gas gauge as it hovered over the E. Slowly the needle climbed. She didn't push her luck; a quarter of a tank ought to do it.

She'd begun at the courthouse, where she'd run into Jimmy and his pack of rowdy friends before, but there had been no sign. She'd found a broken window and a half-empty carton of cigarettes lying beneath a rack of lighters at the drugstore, and felt a spurt of hope; if they'd gotten away with this theft, then perhaps they'd leave it at that.

She didn't want to drive by the garage, but the big boss's words echoed in her mind. *Think about that boy. The rest of his life hangs in the balance.* She had no right to avoid pain herself if it would cost Jimmy.

The garage was dark. So was the room above. Was Dalton sleeping peacefully, relieved that he had escaped an obviously crazy woman?

Stop worrying about yourself, she ordered silently. But the command did nothing to stop the sudden stinging of her eyes.

She wouldn't cry, she told herself fiercely. She hadn't cried in over a hundred years, and she wasn't going to start now. She just wasn't. She was going to stop this nonsense and find Jimmy.

She pulled to the side of the road and shut off the car. She hadn't tried a probing search yet, because of the cost in time and the drain on her energy. It was difficult to do when you didn't know where to aim your thoughts, and had to cover wide areas to find your subject. But she wasn't gaining anything by driving around, chasing wild guesses.

She'd quarter the town, she thought. That made for fairly large areas, but anything smaller, while potentially more accurate, would take more time. She'd do the area around the garage first, then the area around the high school—they might have gone back for more graffiti—then back to the Kirkland's—

No, she'd check the Kirklands' first, just in case Jimmy had shown up back home. Maggie would have no way to reach her. She leaned back in the seat, closed her eyes, and stretched out her senses.

Jimmy hadn't come home. She hadn't really expected it to be that easy, but it had been worth a try. She shifted then, to the area around the garage, probing for the pattern that was unmistakably Jimmy's. She found only the faint, lingering traces left by his frequent presence.

And she found something else, something she hadn't meant to, although she supposed her senses were so attuned to him she couldn't help it. Dalton was gone. The room above the garage was empty.

She sat up a little straighter, her hands instinctively going to the big steering wheel for support. Maggie said she had called him. Was it possible that he, too, was out looking for the boy? Had there been that much softening in that hard, implacable man? Did she dare hope that she'd accomplished at least that, that her time here hadn't been a complete failure?

It's time you stopped thinking about yourself.

The big boss's words rang in her head once again, this time taking on the tone of a tolling bell.

It *was* a bell. The town fire bell, summoning the small volunteer fire department.

An image flashed through her mind, the science teacher beside her, pointing out Allen and another boy. *The two who had been expelled last year for setting the fire in the school library.* Instantly she shifted her target zone, concentrating her efforts on the high school.

She got it almost immediately. The crackle of flames flaring unexpectedly out of control, the insidious, deadly billows of smoke . . . and four frightened boys, caught in a trap of their own making.

She wasn't sure if she'd nudged the Chevy a little, or if the powerful motor had really gotten her there in less than a minute. She didn't even care; she left the car parked crazily and started toward the school buildings at a run. She realized she'd automatically yanked the keys from the ignition, and shoved them into her pocket in irritation at wasting even that precious split second of time. She knew she was faster than any normal person, but she still wished for more speed as she spotted the smoke rising in dark, ominous clouds from the back of the science building, the oldest one at the school.

She heard the sirens of the town's two fire engines, but they seemed much too distant. She went over the six-foot, chain-link fence in a scrambling leap, barely noticing Jimmy's brightly colored bike leaning against it. She came down running. The closer she got, the more vivid the images became. She was reading Jimmy clearly now, was getting his fear and his remorse.

She ran harder, knowing now just how serious the situation was. They'd broken into the chemistry lab with the intention of trashing the place, but the temptation of the old Bunsen burners and the various chemicals and the stolen cigarette lighters had been too much to resist. Now the fire that had followed the explosion they'd managed to create had them trapped in the tiny back storage room, itself dangerously full of more fuel.

The ominous orange light was obvious the moment she turned the corner, lighting the windows with a frightful glow. When she got closer, she could see the flames flaring up, licking at the ceiling of the room.

She knew they had gotten in through a window they'd broken, but she didn't have time to search for it. The sirens were closer now, but it would still take too long for the four boys. The fire was closing in, and she had to get to them.

She went straight to the door, already able to feel the heat from behind it. She knew what would happen when she opened it, so she began to build the protective cloak she would need to get through the flames. She summoned it up swiftly, knowing there was so very little time to waste. The instant she saw that the dim, oddly fluorescent glow had surrounded her, she reached for the doorknob.

It was hot, she was aware of that, but felt no pain. It was also locked, but she gave it a focused look as she turned it; it clicked and gave.

The flames boiled out at her, hungry for the new source of oxygen she'd provided. But the cloak held, and the fire divided around her like a racing stream around a small but stubborn rock. She walked into the inferno.

It was all she could do to maintain the cloak and get through the wreckage of the room. The smoke was black and thick and, with all the chemicals, probably full of noxious fumes, she thought. Dodging the debris of the furnishings made it worse.

By the time she made it to the storage room door, the flames were already there. It would be burned through in seconds, she thought, moving quickly. She used the cloak to hold back the flames until she got inside and shut the door once more.

The boys were huddled on the floor, their eyes wide with fright. All traces of toughness were gone from them now; Allen's face bore the telltale traces of tears.

Jimmy saw her first.

"Ms. Law?" he exclaimed in astonishment, then coughed; the smoke was getting through. The others merely gaped at her as if she were some fire-induced apparition.

"Get down," she ordered them. "In the corner. Close to the floor, where there's more oxygen."

They were already on the floor, but at her command scooted quickly into the corner farthest from the fire and hunkered down even more.

"Face the wall," she ordered again. "Put your arms over your heads. And don't look around. That smoke could be poisonous, with all those chemicals, or it could burn your eyes."

Thoroughly chastened, the boys did as directed without question. When she was certain they weren't looking, she shifted the cloak, moving it from around her and shaping it into a shield to seal off this end of the room. It was a stretch, and she knew she wouldn't be able to hold it for long, but she heard the wailing sirens stop suddenly, close by, and knew the fire department was here. She could only hope they wouldn't take too long to get to this room.

She thought of trying to get through a wall to the outside, but she couldn't relinquish the shield that long; the flames would be on them before she could do it. It was incredibly lucky that all four boys had been in one place; she'd never have been able to save them all if they'd been spread out. She could already feel the draining of her strength—

She felt a soul-deep, heart-wrenching jolt. The shield wobbled for a moment, letting a deadly finger of smoke in before she managed to shut it off.

Dalton.

Oh, God, Dalton. He was here.

It took her a moment to find the balance, to determine how much energy she could spare from the shield to seek him out. And then she heard him, calling for Jimmy. And saw him, heading toward the engulfed building in a limping run. She voiced a split-second prayer that the connection between them was still there, and then reached out.

As it always seemed to be with him, she got a burst of images; she now knew how long he'd wrestled with the incredible story she'd told him, how he'd matched it up to everything that had happened, how he'd remembered every moment of their time together, everything she'd ever said to him, and the way she'd touched him . . . and how he'd felt when she'd told him she loved him.

What she didn't know was if he would hear her. But she knew she had to try.

Dalton, no! Stop!

She sent it with every bit of her strength, risking the momentary loss of the shield, because he was at the door, reaching for it. Then she had to rechannel her energy to the shield, able only to spare enough to see him.

He stopped, his head coming up sharply, and she knew she'd gotten through. *Angie? God, not you, too!*

And then, like a horrifying film played against her eyelids, she saw him charge into the flames.

Dalton, no!

Keep talking, Angie. I'll find you.

Get out! We'll be all right, get out!

Angie—

The message stopped abruptly, and Angie's heightened hearing heard the racking cough as he tried to breathe and got nothing but choking smoke. He had dodged the first wall of fire that was eating away toward the roof, but another was in his path, consuming one of the huge lab tables. Yet he kept coming.

God, Dalton, please! Believe me, we'll be all right! Get out while you can!

Can't... leave you here.

He tried to dodge a downed shelf, but his foot came down on a slippery piece of broken glass and his injured ankle gave way. He went to his knees, and she felt the slicing pain of more glass as if it were her own hands being slashed. But he staggered to his feet and kept coming.

The smoke was thicker now, so thick he was merely a shape moving through it. Even as she thought it, Angie heard him coughing again, steadily, unrelentingly now. Her head began to swim, and it took her a moment to realize it wasn't from the strain of keeping the shield intact, that it was his dizziness she was feeling. He was taking in too much smoke, that awful, thick, noxious smoke....

Turn around, she begged. God, Dalton, go back.

He went down again, this time coughing so fiercely she wrapped her own arms around her ribs in reaction.

Angie...

Agony clawed at her, talons digging deep and twisting. She couldn't extend the shield; it was taking everything she had to keep it going in this small space. She couldn't even spare the energy to call for help from the bosses. She flicked a glance at the boys huddled on the floor, heard

Jimmy trying to keep them calm as if he were the oldest instead of the youngest.

She had no choice. If she tried to help Dalton, they would die.

So instead, he would die.

No! She couldn't let it happen.

She sent him the strongest message she could manage, letting the shield go dangerously thin.

Dalton, get up! Crawl if you have to. I'll tell you which way.

Angie, I—

Just do it!

She saw his shape change through the smoke, then move, and realized he was doing exactly what she'd said. The miracle of it, that he trusted her, that he obviously believed her now, was something she would treasure forever. But later, when he was safe. She put her fingers to her temples to sharpen the smoky picture.

To your left . . . there! Now straight ahead. No, you're veering right . . . that's it.

He was going to make it. She wouldn't let it be any other way.

Keep going . . . watch out for the lab table on your right, it's about to— Dalton!

He went down hard when the blazing table caught his shoulder as it collapsed. She heard his hoarse gasps, and her own lungs burned as he drew in nothing but smoke. He tried to move, but she sensed his grasp on consciousness slipping.

Don't give up!

Can't breathe. . . .

Keep fighting—

She broke off as she realized she was coughing on her own; the shield was slipping. She was spread too thin, she couldn't do both. She had to shut down one or the other.

She shuddered violently, the choice ripping at her, tearing her up in a way she knew would never heal, because it was really no choice at all.

On some other level, her mind went about the business of shoring up the shield. The rest of her mind was numb, shutting down in its inability to face what she had to do.

And then she heard it, weak and faint, but unmistakable.

Love you . . . Ange.

And then she felt nothing except a sudden yawning blackness as Dalton MacKay's valiant spirit gave up the fight.

"I still can't believe it."

The soot-stained fireman who had chopped through the outer wall for a reason he still didn't understand, stared at the little group in awe. They were outside now, the boys still gulping in the fresh air as if they would never get enough, even though the fire had been out for nearly ten minutes. Angie just stared at the smoldering pile of debris.

"It's an absolute miracle," the paramedic who had checked them over agreed.

"Like hell it was."

Both men looked at Angie as she spoke her first words since she'd led the boys through the gaping hole and out into the cool night air. They quickly decided she was referring literally to the flames, and she didn't dispute it; no one would understand bleak, despairing bitterness from someone who had just survived a fire that indeed could have rivaled hell.

Allen and the other two boys, after a last, wondering look at Angie, went off with one of the volunteer fire fighters who was going to watch them until the sheriff got here. She wondered idly if this would have any effect on them, then decided she didn't really care. She stood silently, watching, waiting.

Jimmy lingered, insisting on staying with Angie. He seemed to be in a state of shock, but Angie couldn't find it in her to care about that, either. Her gaze was fastened on the ruins of the classroom.

When two men in yellow slickers at last came out, a stained blanket covering their grim burden, the last flicker of feeling inside her died. She felt more numb, more incapable of emotion than the bosses had ever been able to make her.

"Damn," Jimmy exclaimed, coming out of his daze, staring at the stretcher. "Did somebody die?"

Angie turned on him then.

"Yes, Jimmy, somebody did," she said, her voice making the chill night air seem warm. "He saw your bike outside, knew you were in trouble.... He must have known he didn't have a chance, but he tried. And he died trying to save you."

"But who would do a crazy thing like that? Besides you, I mean...."

His voice trailed away as the other possibility occurred to him. Angie just looked at him. She'd run out of caring, run out of mercy for this boy. Jimmy glanced to where the men were carrying the blanket-covered stretcher toward the back of the parked ambulance that served the coroner. Then he looked back at Angie, his eyes wide with horror, his face pale.

"Not... God, not Dalton?"

Her expression gave him his answer.

"No!" Jimmy yelled, backing away from her as if that would make it not true. She just looked at him, until he knew she wasn't lying.

Jimmy moaned. She didn't care. It meant nothing to her. Nothing did. Nothing except the man they were putting in the back of that ambulance. The man who had shown her what she'd never understood about life, love…and now death. The man who had ripped her heart out and taken it with him when he'd died with a simple declaration of love that had come with his last breath.

She reached into her pocket and dug out the keys to the Chevy. She tossed them at Jimmy, but he was too bewildered to react.

"The car is yours. I don't ever want to see it again." She couldn't bear to. Not with the memories it held.

She heard the slamming of the doors of the ambulance. She didn't look. Jimmy just stared at her in shocked disbelief.

"Dalton died for you, Jimmy Sawyer. He thought you were worth dying for, and I don't want you to ever forget that."

She had no idea how the boy would live with it. Or how she would; she knew deep in her soul that she was the reason Dalton hadn't stopped, hadn't escaped when he could have. He'd been trying to save her. In spite of everything, he had loved her. And died for her.

"You'd damned well better make something out of your life, Jimmy. You owe it to him."

She supposed he would. She could feel the beginnings stirring in him even now. But she didn't care.

She walked back to look one last time at the smoldering ruin. Her eyes searched out the spot where Dalton had collapsed for the last time.

Slowly she reached up and yanked on the pendant, so fiercely, the chain snapped. It thrummed urgently in her hand, as it had been doing ever since she had led the four boys to safety. She ignored it.

With a single, violent motion, she threw the little piece of gold into the ashes.

And then she walked away into the darkness.

Twelve

———

Angie didn't notice the warmth as the sun cleared the mountains, any more than she had noticed the cold during the hours before dawn. She simply sat, enduring, waiting, on this rock overlooking the little town where her understanding of life had begun and ended.

The gently rolling hills, green from the recent rain and dotted here and there with the solitary oak trees that made the grouped three of the town plaza stand out, should have been soothing. They would have been, had she been capable of being soothed.

She didn't even jump when the figure appeared on the hill above her, silhouetted by the slanting rays of the morning sun. She'd been waiting for something like this.

He walked down until he was in front of her, then sat on a boulder barely a foot away. She barely glanced at him. And she couldn't even find it in herself to be amused at the fact that he was dressed as she'd first seen him all those years ago, in the clothes of a Mississippi riverboat gambler—felt hat, brocade vest and all. She supposed it was to remind her of what they'd done for her on the day her family had died. She also supposed she should feel honored; the big boss didn't often leave their equivalent of the ivory tower.

He cleared his throat. And cleared it again. And again. Angie suddenly realized he was having trouble remembering how to talk; the physical act had been unnecessary for them for centuries.

"Ye— Ahem, uh ... You've shut us out, Evangeline."

Yes, she had. She'd sensed them trying to contact her, but without the pendant, she'd been able to block them out. I learned about walls from an expert, she thought.

"You must talk to us, you know."

"Must I?" She looked at him then, wondering that she had ever been intimidated by him.

"Evangeline—"

"You want me to talk? All right, I will. Long enough to ask one question. Why did you let it happen? You're supposed to help, not hurt."

He cleared his throat yet again. And when he spoke, she noticed with a vague sense of surprise—the strongest emotion she'd felt in all the hours since Dalton's death—that he seemed almost embarrassed.

"We must admit," he said, "we haven't quite learned everything about human emotions yet. But you've expanded our knowledge greatly, Evangeline. Although we don't quite understand this odd connection that seemed to develop between you and Mr. MacKay. That was most unusual. And we are sorry you had to experience pain. However, it has—"

"Me?"

Every bit of her agony, her anger, her grief, came roaring back to life in an instant. She rocketed to her feet.

"Do you really think I give a damn about me? You're supposed to do good, isn't that the idea? The generous, all-knowing, benevolent benefactors, isn't that how you see yourselves? Then explain to me why Dalton is just as dead as if you were the devil incarnate, and cruelty your intent from the beginning!"

"Evang—"

"Angie!" she shouted. "My name is Angie. Not that I care what you call me. All I want from you is for you to put me right back where you found me and go away."

"You don't mean that. You would—"

"Die? Yes. But I wouldn't ever have to have anything to do with any of you, ever again. And that would be worth it." She turned her head and stared down the hill into town, thankful the school wasn't visible from here.

He adopted what she assumed was supposed to be a soothing tone. "Don't be hasty, dear. There is much left to be done, and now that you have learned more of people, you should be more efficient. And we have learned, as well, thanks to you. Although this thing humans call love still has us quite amazed."

Her head snapped around. She stared at him for a long moment.

"You let it happen," she whispered in stunned realization. "That's why you stalled about an adjustment. You let me fall in love with Dalton so that you could *study* us! Like a couple of lab rats."

"It wasn't quite that . . . calculating. You were already responding oddly to the man, in spite of our instructions to the contrary. As usual," he added in a mildly censorious tone.

Her eyes widened as another thought occurred to her. "Is that why you ordered me to stay away from him? Because you figured I'd do the opposite?"

"Well, you do have a certain knack for being contrary, my dear. And we truly were not certain how to correct the problem you were having. So we simply took advantage of the situation as a . . . learning opportunity. For you as well as for us."

She felt a pervasive weakness in her knees, and dropped down to sit on the rock again.

"*Us,*" she echoed sarcastically. "Will you drop that absurd royal 'we'? You can't tell me that anyone other than you would make that kind of decision."

"All right, I did, then. Evangeline, he was—"

"I told you, it's Angie."

"Very well, although I don't see why. You've always hated the name."

"Not..." Her anger wavered at the memory of the sweet sound. "Not when Dalton said it."

When he spoke again, the boss's voice was as gentle as she'd ever heard it. "He was already doomed, he'd chosen his path. He would have succumbed eventually, so I didn't think it would do any harm."

"Harm?" Fury rose in her again. "My God, he's dead! How much more harm can there be?"

"No, Angie. He was beyond our help, but at least he's at peace now."

"Your arrogance is boundless, isn't it? Well, let me tell you something, Mr. Boss. You've made one large error in your calculations. There's one thing you still haven't learned about love. You can't turn it off after the experiment is over. And I will love Dalton MacKay for the rest of my life, be it sixty seconds or sixty years."

"Don't worry, dear, we'll suppress those feelings, even the memories, if you like. That's one more thing we've been working on recently—"

"The hell you will! They're all I have of him, and I won't let you take them away. And you were wrong about that, too! He *wasn't* beyond help. He was trying, he'd begun to heal, to feel again. To care again. He died trying to save Jimmy, you bastards."

And he told me he loved me.

"Angie—"

"You still don't get it, do you? He could have saved Jimmy by himself, don't you see? And he would have. It was *me* who wasn't needed here. It's your fault he's dead, because you just don't understand." Her voice broke. "You had no right . . . to let him start to have hope again, and then let his life be snuffed out as if it meant nothing."

Her barriers crumbled then. And Angie, the ever-sassy, ever-argumentative Angie, for the first time in over a hundred years, broke down and sobbed. Violently, helplessly, all of her proud, determined strength gone. And her boss stared at her in shock, in the manner of one who is only now realizing the enormity of his mistake.

Angie sensed him leave, although she didn't look up. She couldn't bear to take even one more look at the world that no longer held the man she loved. She waited, for what seemed like hours, each moment expecting to be flung back in time to where they'd found her, to be back on that side-wheeler deck with the muddy river rising around her, the screams of the dead and dying echoing in her ears, and the pain . . .

She would welcome the pain. Perhaps it would distract her from this soul-deep agony that was so much worse. And it wouldn't be long, she'd been close to death when they'd come to her, but now she would have no reason to fight. She would welcome that, too; if joining him in death was as close as she could get to Dalton, she would accept it gladly.

Her wrenching sobs had subsided to quiet weeping when she felt the soft touch of fingers on her face. Odd, she thought. They'd never touched her, not even when she'd been in training. She'd gotten the idea they were unable to, even when they took on human form. Perhaps they were saying goodbye or—

The fingers had tilted her head back, and she felt the press of warm, gentle lips on her cheeks, kissing away the tears. Startled, her eyes flew open and she rapidly blinked, staring at the man in front of her.

"This is a rotten joke," she snapped. "If you think just because you can manage to look like him—"

"Ange, it's me."

Ange. She'd never told them that. Only Angie.

"Dalton?" she whispered, not daring to believe.

"They pulled me out of...whatever limbo I was in. After the fire. They explained it all. That everything you'd said was true. And that they'd made a big mistake, and were about to lose you...over me."

"Dalton," she said again, lifting a hand to touch him, to trace his jaw, his chin, his lips with her fingers, heedless of their trembling. He pulled her into his arms then, and she heard the steady thud of his heart beneath her cheek. The heart she'd thought stilled for eternity.

"They told me if I still felt guilty about Mick, they were going to give me a chance to make up for it, by doing what you do. But I told them you'd already made me see that I wasn't really responsible for the accident that day."

"After—" the booming voice came unexpectedly from behind them; the big boss had condescended to once more come out of his tower "—he 'read me the riot act,' as you

so quaintly put it, for putting you in the position of having to choose between those boys and the man you loved.''

"You deserved it," Dalton said flatly. "She went
through hell.''

"You believed me," Angie said, her voice full of wonder and joy at how far he'd come. He'd faced down the
most intimidating being she'd ever confronted, for her.
Immediately Dalton turned back to her.

"Yes, I believed you. I just had to work my way through
a lot of things." His mouth quirked in that way she so
loved. "That was a hell of a story you told me."

Angie moved then, hugging him fiercely, thrilling to the
feel of him, solid and alive and unscarred, in her arms.

"I must say," the big boss grumbled, "humans are *most*
unpredictable. I made the mistake of telling him we
couldn't afford to lose you. So what did he do?"

Angie, still lost in the wondrous discovery that Dalton
was truly with her, and that he loved her, didn't even look
at the boss as she asked, "What did he do?"

"He bargained with me. With *me!*" Angie nearly smiled
at his outrage. "He told me we got both of you, together,
or neither. And that he had something he had to be able to
do first.''

Angie looked into Dalton's eyes then, curiously. And
saw the answer there. "Linda?" she said softly.

Dalton lowered his eyes and nodded. "I . . . she deserves
to know I'm all right. I never thought about it that way,
until you made me see that, too. They told me I'd be able
to make her feel all right about it."

Angie's throat tightened; he'd come so far, so fast, this
man they'd written off as doomed.

The boss coughed, an irritated little sound. "You mean
you coerced me into breaking a cardinal rule." He shook
his head in a creditable imitation of exasperation. He

glanced at Angie. "I can see already that he is going to be as big a problem as you are."

Angie was busy drinking in the sight and feel of the boss's newest problem child, and didn't say a word.

"However," the boss went on, never at a loss for words. "I can see some advantages to this arrangement. There are times when a pair of operatives who could go in as a couple would be quite useful."

"And?" Dalton prompted. "There's one more part to the deal, if you recall?"

The boss looked puzzled, then his expression cleared. "Hmm, er, yes. I believe I owe you what you call an apology, Evangel—Angie. I misjudged the situation from the beginning. And I once more underestimated the power of human emotions."

"Once more?" she asked, glancing at him curiously. "You mean something like this has happened before?"

"Er, yes. It's a very long story."

"We have lots of time, now," she said sweetly.

"Later," the boss said gruffly. He reached into the pocket of his out-of-time brocade vest. "I believe you . . . forgot this." He held up the gold steamboat.

Angie winced at the reminder of the agony she'd been in at that moment. And immediately the boss's hand curled around the pendant. An odd, golden glow seeped from between his fingers. After a moment he opened them, checked what he held, and smiled in satisfaction.

"I think you may find these of more use now. I'm getting quite good at this."

Both Angie and Dalton stared down at the simple yet incredibly lustrous gold rings that lay on his palm. He tossed the rings at Dalton, who caught them with a quick snap of his wrist. Dalton shifted his gaze to Angie's face.

When he spoke, he sounded as if he were holding his breath.

"Angie? Will you?"

"Of course," she said, taking Dalton's hands in hers. "I love you."

She saw him swallow tightly. "I love you, too."

"I know. You told me."

His brows furrowed. "I never had the chance, after I finally worked things through, but—" He stopped, his eyes widening. "You mean . . . in the fire?"

"Yes."

He let out a breath. "I didn't think you got it. The last thing I remember thinking was that you'd never know. . . ."

He swallowed tightly, and she hugged him again.

"I knew. It's all right now. Everything will be all right."

"Thank goodness," the boss said wryly. "At least we won't be losing another one to this amazing affliction."

"Someday I want that other story," Angie said. But her eyes never left Dalton's face. His beautiful, now unscarred face.

"Perhaps," the boss said, and quickly changed the subject. "You'll have to take her name, you know," he told Dalton. "At least for a while."

"I'll take it forever," Dalton answered, looking only at Angie. "In anyone's kind of time."

"Only because the name Dalton MacKay's still well known—" the boss was still explaining "—and as far as the world knows, he died in that fire."

"Thank you for the rings," Angie said politely but dismissively, her gaze fastened on the beloved green eyes she'd thought never to see again.

"Well, I did owe you something—"

"You still do," Dalton said. "So don't forget that little item we're going to negotiate later."

"Yes, er, well—"

"What item?" Angie asked, amused at the big boss's disconcertedness, but not enough to look away from Dalton.

"Babies," Dalton said succinctly.

"Oh," Angie said, color tinging her cheeks. Had he read her in that moment when she had longed for his child? Whatever the reason, she was glad. "Oh, yes."

"Well—" the big boss actually coughed "—I suppose we can work something out...."

"Good," Dalton said. "Now go away."

"Excuse me?"

Dalton didn't answer. Neither did Angie. They were savoring the kiss they'd never thought to have. And it didn't appear they had any intention of stopping with merely a kiss.

For the first time in his lengthy existence, the big boss felt utterly superfluous. "Someday," he muttered, "I'll understand this." But he knew when he'd worn out his welcome, and after weaving a protective shell around the oblivious couple, he said benevolently, "Later, children," and vanished.

As they went down to the sweet bed of grass that had mysteriously appeared at their feet, neither Dalton nor Angie even noticed he was gone. Or heard his pleased laughter floating on the breeze.

*   *   *   *   *

SILHOUETTE

Desire

COMING NEXT MONTH

MYSTERIOUS MOUNTAIN MAN
Annette Broadrick

Man of the Month

Rebecca Adams needed Jake Taggart. Only he could save her company. But he was living halfway up a mountain and she was going to have to go and get him. They'd be alone in the wilderness…

IMPULSE
Lass Small

Amy Allen took one look at Chas Cougar and decided she just had to meet him, so she decided to pose as a distant cousin and gate-crash the wedding he was attending. Chas knew right away Amy wasn't kin, but he could change that…if she was willing to be wed!

THE COP AND THE CHORUS GIRL
Nancy Martin

Opposites Attract

A cop couldn't ignore a female in distress, but it was unusual for a bride to rush away from the church before the wedding, which was why Patrick Flynn didn't react as quickly as Dixie wanted. Now he was going to have to fight off her gangster groom.

COMING NEXT MONTH

DREAM WEDDING
Pamela Macaluso

Just Married

Once Alex would have sold his soul to kiss Genie. Now his "dream girl" was a prim teacher and the swot she'd rejected, who'd turned into a strapping, sexy CEO, was back for revenge.

HEAVEN CAN'T WAIT
Linda Turner

Spellbound

Prudence Sullivan knew Zeb Murdock was the lover for whom she'd waited centuries. Unfortunately, although he felt the fire between them, Murdock was determined to resist her. Pru couldn't allow that!

FORSAKEN FATHER
Kelly Jamison

Rachel Tucker had to resist rekindling the past—or risk revealing the secret she should have told John McClennon years ago. She had to protect her son.

COMING NEXT MONTH FROM

▼ SILHOUETTE

Sensation

A thrilling mix of passion, adventure and drama

RESTLESS WIND Nikki Benjamin
POINT OF NO RETURN Rachel Lee
NIGHTSHADE Nora Roberts
STILL MARRIED Diana Whitney

Intrigue

*Danger, deception and desire—
new from Silhouette...*

UNDER THE KNIFE Tess Gerritsen
RISKY BUSINESS M.J. Rodgers
GUILTY AS SIN Cathy Gillen Thacker
PRIVATE EYES Madeline St. Claire

Special Edition

Satisfying romances packed with emotion

A MAN FOR MUM Gina Ferris Wilkins
A SECRET AND A BRIDAL PLEDGE Andrea Edwards
DOES ANYONE KNOW WHO ALLISON IS?
Tracy Sinclair
TRULY MARRIED Phyllis Halldorson
A STRANGER IN THE FAMILY Patricia McLinn
A PERFECT SURPRISE Caroline Peak